Nero

ISBN: 978-1-9194540-0-9

Cover Design: Chris Reilly (Deposit Photos/Canva)
Interior Format: Chris Reilly Author

NERO

BOOK 1 BLACKHAWK DISCIPLES MC

CHRIS REILLY

About The Series

The Blackhawk Disciples MC is a 10-book series. Each book focuses on a single couple who have their HEA within the book.

The overarching storyline will run through the full series and must be read in order. All the brothers of the MC appear in every book.

Trigger Warnings

This series has darker themes including, violence and death and deals with grief from parental loss. Further trigger warnings for the series can be found on my website www.chrisauthorreilly.com

Chapter One

Nero

"Take him to the farm and finish it."

"We haven't got anything useful out of him," Rebel, my Vice President says.

I get why he's pissed, I feel it too. This asshole, Dutton, was supposed to give us a lead on who is trying to undermine my club. He hasn't broken yet, and with my long history of handling this kind of situation, I know he won't. He's done, and we're wasting our time.

No one else knows I discovered this sorry piece of shit murdered a woman when he was in college, or that woman's brother is attached to my MC. It isn't relevant to the situation my club is in now, so I will keep it to myself. The fucker deserves to die, that's all that matters.

"And we're not going to," I tell Rebel, then look at each of the other men in turn, letting them know this decision is final. "Get him out of my sight."

He'll be taken to Stryker's pig farm. The thought of that place leaves a nasty taste in my mouth, but it serves a purpose. Particularly when shit like this happens. The truth of it is, it's never failed me yet and has kept the club safe over the years, no matter how disgusting it is.

The pointed silence from the men watching me comes from a place of respect and knowing where they stand in this MC. What I say goes, everyone knows that.

Dammit, I'm fucking tired. God knows I'm never fully able to switch off. It comes with the territory of being the President. It's been nonstop for weeks, but for now, this road has hit a dead end. What comes next can be dealt with tomorrow.

Rebel is the only one who looks at me like he wants to have a serious fucking word. It will come but not now. I spare one last look at the sorry excuse for a man, then head out of the warehouse where we brought him to get some answers.

My VP may be against this decision, but only he fully understands the maneuvers I'm constantly making to keep this city safe. The people I pay off, bribe and make deals with behind the scenes. The civilians around the club need to be safe.

I'm not an idiot. There are certain dangers our club being in the community can bring. But I'll be damned if it spills over into the lives of the normal people in my city. I have done my best to integrate us into the community. So far, it's worked, and we have no trouble.

When my house comes into view, I breathe a little easier. There is something more important to me than the Blackhawk Disciples here. If you told me I would make that statement a few years ago, I'd have punched you in the face and threatened to break your neck.

Inside this house is my reason for living. My life changed in ways I'll never be able to describe the second I found out about him.

It pains me to think of him as a complication. It left me reeling for weeks when I found out I had a son. There is no way to describe the emotions that went through me. Shock, to anger, to wonder, to love, back to anger. At her. Never my boy.

I'm a rational man, and ultimately, I'm thankful she came to me after giving birth. She could have kept him a secret, like she did with the pregnancy. I could have gone through life never knowing I had a child.

That is what I cling to the most. Hating my son's mother will only harm him.

We get along, living separately, sharing custody, with an understanding she never tells a soul who he is to me. Loving him could be used against me, and I will never put him in that position.

Everything was going fine until shit went sideways when Sheridan showed up two weeks ago and left him with me, because she *wasn't coping*.

After parking the bike at the far end of the drive, I slip into the house through the back door. Jesse is in the kitchen stirring a pot on the stove, the smell makes my stomach knot, reminding me that in all the excitement tonight, I've not eaten.

"Hey," Jesse isn't surprised by my appearance at the back door, used to my comings and goings at all hours of the day and night. "Everything okay?"

"Fine," I lie. Jesse knows I'm lying, but club business stays between members. "How is he?"

"It took a while to put him down, but he's sleeping now."

"What was the problem?" That inherent worry that comes from being a parent kicks in.

"Sheer stubbornness."

I eye Jesse, wanting to know what the fuck that means, then remember my son is more like me than I'd like to admit. Two-years-old, and he knows exactly what he wants and isn't afraid to demand it. He's a good kid, smart too. He's going through some changes, what with his mom running off. I've struggled to get him to sleep myself.

"You don't need me in the morning, right?" Jesse asks.

Fuck, given what went down tonight, I'll need to get back to the clubhouse early. Jesse sees it and frowns. I've known Jesse my whole life. We grew up on the same street. He was fascinated with my family's way of life, but never aspired to join the MC. Not that Crash, the previous president, would have let him.

From a very young age, it was clear Jesse was into guys. His sexual orientation never bothered me, but it wasn't welcome at the Club. Now I run the place, things are different. Some of the old timers didn't like it when I changed shit up, but I am in charge. What I say goes.

Anyone who doesn't like it, they're free to fuck right off. People have a right to be whoever they want to be, and unless they're a raging asshole or a complete fuckwit, I'm not going to judge them. No one left, but I keep my eye on those who don't like it.

By the time I was running the place, Jesse had gotten a business degree in college and opened his own financial consultancy agency.

Over the years, it's grown bigger both in size and reputation, and now he is CEO of a highly sought-after finance company.

Jesse was as shocked as I was finding out about Oscar, but he stepped up, knowing I couldn't take care of my son the way a normal father does. They're like two peas in a pod. Sometimes I watch them and think my son loves Jesse more than me, and guilt wracks me.

Jesse will never let Oscar forget I'm his dad.

"I have an appointment. It'll only take a couple of hours. I can be back around lunchtime."

My gut plummets. "What's wrong?"

"It's routine." He watches my jaw clench and rolls his eyes. "I'd say if something was wrong."

"I haven't forgotten the time you thought you were going fucking blind and didn't tell me shit."

He turns off the burner and moves the pan to the counter, saying nothing as he grabs a bowl and scoops some of the stew into it. Anyone witnessing this would think he was my fucking husband. I'm too hungry to care. I'm also not letting this drop.

"You don't go to the clinic unless there is a problem."

"Christ, Noah. I'm fine." Jesse never calls me by my road name. We've known each other too long for that. It also sounds weird as shit whenever he calls me Nero.

My eyes narrow. "Are you overdoing it? Getting too tired?"

"This isn't about Oscar," he snaps. "Keeping active is one thing that is good for me." He shoves the bowl across the counter at me, together with a wedge of sourdough bread. "I don't want to discuss it."

If anyone in the club could see me now, they wouldn't recognize me. The worry is written all over my face when normally I control my emotions. People think I'm an unfeeling bastard.

"Are you taking your insulin properly?"

"Of course I am."

"So what the fuck is up?"

"Will you give it a damn rest? And stop cussing at me."

Losing Jesse is not up for debate. Yes, I agree he takes care of himself. There has never been any worry, not really. The whole going blind thing was blurry vision that was corrected with dosage changes of his medication.

"I'm going home."

He heads around the counter but stops in front of me. "I don't want to talk about the symptoms I'm experiencing right now because it's personal and you won't want to hear it."

Everything there is to know about diabetes is imprinted on my brain. All the complications, all the issues he lives with. I can't help it, my eyes drop to his crotch. Not in a pervy way, but if he doesn't want to discuss it, then it's got to be something to do with that.

Without warning, Jesse punches me. He has a mean right hook and catches my jaw. I snarl at him, but don't hit him back. It wasn't even hard, he's making a point. This is the way we are with each other. Anyone else tried that, they'd be on the ground in a heartbeat.

Truth is, I don't need to hear about his sex drive. It would make both of us uncomfortable. I can understand why it's bothering him. No guy wants their dick to stop working. Even if I don't like the dickhead he's been dating lately. Somehow, I know that prick would up and walk out on him if shit got bad. Jesse deserves better.

One of my men, Ghost ran a full background check on the guy for me when they first started dating, which came back clean. I still don't trust him, he has a shitty job and rides on Jesse's success more than I like.

Jesse tells me he'll be here around midday, to eat the damn food, and focus on Oscar. Can't argue with that.

I watch him leave then stare at the food he made me, suddenly not all that hungry anymore, but I eat it anyway because he's right, I need to be on top of things tomorrow. Knowing my son, he'll be awake before six AM.

After clearing up, I head upstairs and go check on Oscar. I'm grateful to Sheridan for bringing him into my life. The love I have for this tiny person goes beyond anything else I've ever experienced.

I hate that I'm keeping him a secret, but it's for his own good. No one will ever harm my boy. I'd rain down hell on anyone who even tried. Careful not to disturb him, I go to my room, holding the baby monitor so I can keep an eye on him.

I need a shower and about nine hours of sleep. I won't get either, but what's new? This is my life.

A text comes through as I lay down, so I check the phone. It's Rebel, letting me know the ugly business at Stryker's is done. I send a one-word reply, then set the phone down and stare at the ceiling.

It takes a long time for sleep to take me.

Chapter Two

Taylor

I'm jolted from my thoughts by the loud snap of my name. "Taylor?"

Not sure how long she's been calling me, I suspect it's probably been a few times. I look up at Shannon, the senior nurse on duty who is frowning at me. Not in anger, it's concern.

It takes a moment to pull out of the haze I went into. "Sorry, what did you say?"

"Your patient is here. Ashlyn said she called you, but you didn't pick up."

"I didn't hear the phone." I reach over and pick it up, and there is a dial tone. Shit. I'm supposed to be convincing Shannon I'm fine and ready to be back at work. Not drifting off into memories that keep filling my mind.

"Are you sure you're ready for this?" Shannon moves closer to the desk. "You can take more time off after what you've been through these past few months."

She's not the only person at the clinic who thinks I came back too soon, but what else was I supposed to do? Sit at home and stare at the empty rooms that used to be so full of life? Cry myself into a stupor and wake up looking like I've been hit by a truck.

That has happened more than once. Dad would hate to see me like that. The only way I can keep myself from sinking into depression is to stay busy. Not that Shannon has kept me all that busy since I came back. I've barely seen any patients, instead working on waiting lists and appointments, or doing admin tasks that either Ashlyn our receptionist can do, or Danica, the actual clinic manager.

It's only been two months since I lost my dad. Cancer took him from me. Being a nurse doesn't help. You never expect it, not when cancer decides to take root and destroy your body.

My dad was my best friend. Everyone loved him, he always had time for people, even when he was too busy. That was his way. Selfless. He raised me alone after my mother decided motherhood wasn't for her. We were a team, he was my biggest supporter, my confidante. I'd gone off to college and had my own place, but I never thought of anywhere but Dad's house as home.

It's still hard to comprehend that he is no longer in the world. I've never believed in a higher power, or any kind of deity in the sky. Not until now. I can't bear to think he ceased to exist. He was larger than life. Nothing about him being gone is right.

I'm not sure I'll ever stop missing him. Or the things he used to do that I took for granted. The sound of him yelling at the TV when his baseball team, the Baltimore Orioles, was playing.

Or the never-ending supply of Cocoa Pops cereal he always had in the pantry. The proper kind from the UK, not the plastic, tasteless crap, as he referred to the version made here. He got it shipped over.

I don't even know where he got it from, and the thought of it running out guts me.

"I'm sorry, I got lost in thought," I say, getting up.

"Mr. Cartwright is ready to see you, so long as you're sure. Caitlin can take him if you need time."

Coming around the desk, I pat Shannon's arm. She's in her late forties and has been a mother figure to most of the other nurses under her. She's highly experienced and spent a lot of time in busy ER departments throughout her career. Some in high-risk areas where there was barely any let-up in the violent crimes that saw people ending up in hospital.

She decided to move away from that and into the private nursing business. I'd started out here, so had no clue what it was like doing what Shannon had done before. My aunt suffered with diabetes most of her life, and I love her almost as much as Dad, so when I went into nursing, that was what I specialized in.

I'm lucky to have found my place here. I can't blow it now. Not that I wouldn't be forgiven for taking a little longer away. I just can't. I need to be here.

The last few months of my life have been miserable as fuck. I need some light. If that comes as being around colleagues and patients I've been seeing for the last four years, then this is where I'm going to be.

"It's not doing me any good to stay at home."

"Are you still at his place?"

"Yeah, I let my apartment lease lapse."

"Hey," Caitlyn appears in the doorway before Shannon can ask any more questions. She is a good friend of mine and a fellow nurse at the clinic. "Guess who's here?"

Shannon side-eyes Caitlyn, who gives her a sheepish grin.

"Don't even pretend you don't look forward to his appointments," she tells our boss.

Shannon tries to look stern, but fails miserably. Everyone here loves Jesse Cartwright. Not only is he a lovely guy who is always upbeat and wants to talk to everyone, he's absolutely stunning to look at. Which is irrelevant because he's a patient.

My patient, who I've kept waiting because I went into a fugue state when I'm supposed to be proving to my boss I am ready to be back here.

Jesse is sitting in the back of the waiting area when I head out, frowning at his phone. He doesn't hear me call his name, so I head over.

"Hey, Jesse."

"Oh," he puts his phone away and gives me a dazzling smile. "Sorry, Taylor. Business emails. Why do some people seem to lose their minds if you're out of contact for a couple of hours?"

I recognize that look, that forced smile. It's the look of someone going through something they don't want to talk about. "Maybe you're just that awesome," I grin.

He lets out a small laugh that sounds more like him. We head to my room, and I note Caitlin and Ashlyn staring as we pass.

"How've you been?" he asks

"Good, thanks."

Discussing my personal life with patients doesn't happen. They have enough on their plate without hearing my story. Jesse is the exception. We talked about my dad's battle with cancer a time or two. I always steered the conversation back to his care, though.

It's been two months since I last saw Jesse for a check-up. He doesn't know about Dad. Getting used to telling people you've lost someone isn't something I've got a handle on yet. Fortunately, he doesn't ask as we go into my room.

He looks pensive again and uncomfortable. Not the Jesse I've come to know.

"We're not scheduled for a routine review. Is there something wrong?"

"Everything is going great. Blood sugars are good, taking my medication perfectly. Health wise, I'm great. I'm even signed up for a half marathon in a couple of months, I've been training."

"That's great, I'm glad you're keeping healthy. It's always lovely to hear of people working towards their goals. And a half marathon is no mean feat."

"It's tough, but I've had a lot of reasons to get out and run."

One thing I am not is a therapist. I don't have the tools to counsel people, but I am a compassionate person, a good listener and, fortunately, in a position to signpost if people have issues beyond my scope of understanding. Jesse is the kind of guy you want to help, but not be shortchanged.

"For a little while now, I've been having some... issues?" He says it as if it's a question. I dip my head silently, telling him to go on. "With my libido, I guess."

"Okay, and by issues, what exactly is the concern?"

"Erectile dysfunction."

"Don't self-diagnose. You're young, healthy and your medication levels are great. You don't meet the regular statistics for ED. Do you want to discuss symptoms?"

"I can't get it up," he laughs, though it's strained.

"There can be many reasons for that, so you shouldn't automatically jump to conclusions."

"Like what? Because I've broken the cardinal sin, Taylor. I've researched it online."

"*No*. Online is a bad word here. And what did that get you?"

"My dick is broken, and I'll only be able to get it up by taking a little blue pill that can give me a stiffy for hours on end."

"Jesse," I shake my head.

"I know," he leans back, slapping his hands on his thighs. "I gave myself a stern talking to."

"How much detail do you want to give me so we can figure this out?"

"It's not that I don't want to, when we try it... hides."

Oh God, it is really hard not to laugh. He's using jokes to make light of it, but deep down this is bothering him. I get it, most men who come through here with these kinds of problems find it difficult to be serious. It's all born of fear.

"There are few factors to consider, we've eliminated most of them already. I think the one you may need to explore is the psychological element."

"I need a shrink?"

"Not necessarily. But you may need to explore your feelings about the act of sex. The person you're with, outside factors like work-related stress. You told me that people at work are bothering you when you're not there. It all adds up. Stress on the mind can manifest in physiological ways."

"You're not a therapist, I get that. I needed someone professional to tell me this isn't something I'm going to have to deal with."

"No, I'm not, and I can refer you on to someone who specializes in this and can help you talk things through. If you're not ready for that step," I add, because he looks the furthest thing from wanting to see a therapist. "Then ask yourself what usually brings you to the point of getting erect and what's changed to prevent it."

His cheeks pinked slightly, but he nods. "I'm overreacting, I know that."

"Nothing is an overreaction, Jesse. If it's a genuine concern, I'm here to help. I don't want to overstep, but the person you're with, is it a serious, committed relationship?" He sits in silence. "I'll take that as a you're not sure where you stand kind of response."

"It's new, and I guess there are no big feelings about him."

"But you've been actively having sex until now."

"Yeah."

"And your sex drive is low, medium, high?"

"High usually."

"As a non-sex therapist, I don't want you to take this as an accurate description of the problem, Jesse. I would recommend that you seek advice from a specialist on this. Maybe you need to re-evaluate your personal wants and needs before you factor in something as large as a relationship. Sometimes, we don't connect, or it becomes perfunctory. That could be having an effect."

He stares at the wall for a moment. We sit in silence as he articulates what he wants to say.

"What if I like someone else?"

"Is that something you could explore?"

"Absolutely not."

Damn, now I feel bad. He has feelings for someone else who isn't interested. Like seriously not interested if that vehement statement is anything to go by.

"I wouldn't want to say that's the cause."

"You're being very diplomatic, Taylor. Both of them are wrong for me, that's the problem. I should break up with him and focus on myself. Forget what I can't have."

"At some point in our lives, we all have to do that. It's difficult, but taking care of your own mental health and your actual health, given your condition, should come first."

"You're right. God, what would I do without you?"

"You'd manage," I smile. "Do you want to talk some more, or can I signpost you to some places? I could give you reputable places to do a bit of research. Instead of the damn internet?"

Jesse agrees to the signposting. He looks at his watch and says he needs to get back to work with a roll of his eyes. I walk him to the door and lightly pat his arm.

"I'm here if you need to talk, you can come in anytime."

"Thanks, Taylor. I appreciate that. It's helped to talk about it with someone who understands."

"I'm glad I could help."

We say goodbye, and Jesse heads out. People probably look at him and think he has it all. Underneath the surface, we all have our issues, some more serious than others. I think this is definitely his own head getting in the way. If you're no longer attracted to someone, it's gonna be hard to do the deed with them.

"Taylor?" Ashlyn breaks me out of my thoughts. "Jesse was your last patient, Shannon asked me to see if you were alright, to help with the patient waiting list and bookings?"

Riveting stuff. I agreed to this slow return, so I smile and head behind the reception desk. It's best if I'm around people right now. And while I'm working on bookings, I can slot myself in a few extra patients. What Shannon doesn't know won't hurt her.

I'm barely getting started when Jesse comes back into the clinic. He looks frazzled, his usually perfect hair is sticking up like he's run his hands through it, and not in a good way. I get up and walk around the counter.

"Is everything okay?"

"No. My car won't start, the people at my insurance company are useless, and the towing company can't get here for three hours. I need to get back. Could you hold on to my keys and call me when they show up? I need to Uber back, but there are no cars in the area."

"Of course, we can handle the tow company for you." I take the keys from him. "Are you okay?"

"Yeah, just the whole stress thing." He gives me a tight smile. "I'm running late."

The clinic is quiet, Ashlyn has a handle on the paperwork, despite asking for my help. It's Shannon's way of keeping me here but not overdoing it.

"How about I give you a ride, will that help?"

"You don't have to do that."

"It's fine. I'm due a lunch break anyway. And I'd rather help you out than sit in my room eating stale cracker bread."

"That's not very healthy of you, Nurse."

"See, you're saving me from myself. Let me get my keys."

"You're a lifesaver. I owe you."

"You haven't seen her drive," Ashlyn says.

"Very funny."

"I'd take a ride from an F1 driver right now," Jesse laughs.

"We keep crash helmets in the back."

"It's not that bad," I protest.

Ashlyn and Jesse both laugh. It's good to see a smile on his face. If I can take away some of his worry, then today has been a good day.

Chapter Three

Taylor

The directions he gives me are to one of the nicer neighborhoods in Baltimore, which I kind of expected, given the way Jesse holds himself. I shouldn't make assumptions. He can be the nicest person in the world and live in the shittiest of neighborhoods.

It takes about fifteen minutes to get there. He has five bags of groceries, which we transferred from his trunk to mine, so I get out to help.

"I should be fine if you help me unload them."

Jesse tries to get all the bags at once, and I pat his arm, taking two away from him.

"Okay, thanks, by the front door is fine."

That's good with me. We may know each other at the clinic, but technically I'm still a stranger, he doesn't want me in his house. I'd thought we were going to his office but didn't question him when he gave me the residential address.

We head up the path, and as we approach it, the door is pulled open, and a man steps out.

"Where the hell have you been?" he snaps.

This is who he lives with? No wonder he's having issues getting intimate with him. Aside from the way he looks, which I'm feeling all kinds of guilty about, given my discussion with Jesse, and that he is clearly an asshole. The guy is hot. Even hotter than Jesse, and that is saying something. Not wearing a shirt isn't helping.

He has a gorgeous body, with tattoos covering his chest and arms. A gold chain is resting between his impressive pec muscles, sparkling in the sunlight.

His short hair makes his face more appealing, showing off all the angles and perfect symmetry, and his piercing dark blue eyes are framed with thick lashes.

My impression swerves from *he's so hot it's hard to breathe* to *what an absolute asshole*, in two seconds flat.

"My car broke down. Taylor offered me a ride. Can you move? This stuff is heavy?" Jesse steps through the front door, making the half-naked asshole move out of the way.

I'm not a fan of bullies and worried about Jesse being around this guy. Without waiting for an invitation, I follow him into the house carrying the other two bags. Like I could take this guy if he started anything. He's well over six feet and could likely bench press me with one hand.

"What are you doing?" he calls after me.

"Helping Jesse." I don't even bother to look back, following Jesse down the hall.

"You can't barge in here." The sound of the door slamming makes me flinch, but I don't stop.

Jesse looks up as I come in, he eyes the man behind me and I expect there to be some trepidation, but if anything, there is an amused glint in his eye.

Shit, what have I walked into? I mean, how well do I really know Jesse? The other man storms into the room and comes around to face me. He glares at Jesse as I place the bags on the kitchen island.

"What the hell, Jesse? You can't bring people in here like this." He stares at me. For a moment he pauses, his eyes moving over my face, then down to my scrubs, and back up again.

Is he checking me out? He's an even bigger asshole than I thought. He opens his mouth to say something else when a shout comes from behind him. A toddler wearing red shorts and an adorable teddy bear T-shirt is half crawling, half stumbling into the room.

"Dada, dada," he is calling on repeat.

My head whips from Jesse back to the new guy. Which one of these men is this gorgeous little boy's father? Jesse was in such a hurry to get back. This must be why. But Jesse doesn't make a move towards the child, he carries on getting the groceries out of the bags.

The sharp, *'fuck'* muttered under the other guys' breath, which is no way to talk in front of a small child, surprises me. *He's* his dad? He scoops the kid up and sits his little butt on his forearm.

There is this famous image from decades ago that I remember seeing once. A topless man cradling a baby. This is different, in that this guy has an angry face and is covered in tattoos, and the kid looks to be about two rather than a newborn. But it's painting one hell of a picture in my head.

Stop staring at his chest, for God's sake. I'm looking at the tattoos, that's all. He's a living canvas, wrapped up in an angry, mean package. I keep my face carefully blank. This guy is probably used to women falling at his feet. Or men. I can't forget this is the man who is making Jesse miserable.

The little boy laughs and slaps his face. I like this kid already, although the guy doesn't even flinch. He is still throwing daggers with his eyes in my direction.

His expression does a complete one eighty when he talks to the kid.

"What do you need?" he asks.

"Gingerbees," the kid says. A stern look from his father has him adding on a loud *please*.

Jesse tosses a small, colorful packet of gingerbread men, which the man catches with one hand. It's like they've been doing this for years.

Here I am ogling the guy and he's with Jesse. The guy who is causing him no end of pain to the point it's affecting his body. All I want to do is ask him why he is being such a jerk to the wonderful man behind me. What am I doing? I can't think like this, let alone say it aloud.

"Why are you here?" he snaps.

I slowly turn to face him. He's looking me up and down again, then turns to Jesse, a frown creasing his brow. Now he looks, concerned?

"I'll let you know when the tow company arrives, Jesse," I tell him, turning my back on the man. "Sorry if I caused any issues here," I add quietly.

"Ignore him," he smiles. "That is his permanent state of being."

A quick glance back shows the man settling the boy in a playpen with his treats. He looks up and our eyes meet. The annoyance is back. Jeez, it's not my fault. All I did was help a guy out.

"Thanks, Taylor. I'd have been totally screwed without you. I wouldn't have got back in time," he adds loudly enough that everyone in the room hears.

"Wait," the other guy calls, storming back over.

It takes a lot not to take a step back, he's so big, so intimidating. Jesse puts his hands on his hips and glares back at him.

"Noah, will you calm down?"

Noah. Somehow, that name doesn't seem to fit. I'm not sure why. It's a nice name. Noah's are nice. Not like this ass.

"You need to forget what you saw here."

"Believe me, I intend to forget *you*," I smart back at him.

"Can we not be rude to the lady who helped us both out?"

"You know I don't let people in here," he snaps at Jesse again. The whole time, his dark eyes have been burning into me.

"Jesse, are you okay?" I ask him, wondering what is going on and if Jesse is safe.

"What the fuck is that supposed to mean?" Noah folds his arms over his chest, glowering even hotter than before. "What are trying to say?"

"I'm good, thank you," Jesse says before I can respond.

He's grinning like this is the most fun he's had in ages. I'm lost with this dynamic. This is the guy Jesse was talking about in the clinic. Oh...wait. The other guy?

"We should let you get back to work," Jesse pointedly looks over my shoulder.

I get it, he's hot. And completely unattainable to Jesse it seems. Though I'm not sure why he wants him, or why anyone would. And who on earth procreated with him? And why does a hot rush of jealousy sweep through me at that thought?

"Are you're sure you're alright?" I'm still worried.

"Positive." He maintains the grin. "Noah appreciates you helping me out, too. He isn't good at showing anything other than his raging grumpiness."

"Fucks sake," Noah groans. "Will you just leave."

How dare he? No one has ever spoken to me like this before. I don't even grace him with a look, never mind a response.

"Have a good day, Jesse," I smile, then look at Noah. My mouth takes over against my will. "And you, I hope you have the day you deserve. A crappy one."

Jesse's laughter follows me along the hallway to the front door.

"I'm sorry about him," he says, catching up to me. "He's normally not that bad, he isn't good with strangers. Especially around Oscar."

"It's not like I came in there threatening anyone," I mutter.

"He has his reasons."

I'm not sure I like him making excuses for the guy. One quick glance over his shoulder and I see the asshole watching us.

When I look back at Jesse, I try not to let on that I know this is the guy he wants. Jesse's eyes get real big and he takes a short step back.

"Oh no, no," he puts a hand on my forearm. "Not what we were talking about before."

"Not even the..." God I should stop, this is none of my business.

Jesse pulls a face. "Oh hell no. I tolerate him as a best friend, definitely nothing else."

"Sorry. I shouldn't jump to conclusions, and I shouldn't be bringing up what we discussed in our private appointment."

"It's okay. I can understand why you would think that but no, he's a whole other complication in life, not one that affects my health."

"He's pretty darn nosey too," I nod behind him, making a point of speaking loud enough.

"I heard that," he narrows his eyes at us.

"You were supposed to. Sorry," I say to Jesse.

"Ah, you've got nothing to be sorry about, if anything this has entertained me. Thanks again for the ride. And please call me when they come for the car. I'll get back as soon as I can."

Jesse thanks me again and goes back inside. That was one of the weirdest interactions I've had in... well, ever.

I hope to hell I never have to see that big assbutt again.

On the drive back, I think about where my life is going. What better time to have a full life do over, when one of the biggest parts of it has gone? I've been putting off seeing friends, I'm still not fully back on board at work. Seeing Jesse has gone a long way to waking up my love of my job though.

I hope I helped. In some small way. Nope, not going to let the other one into my brain. Even with all those muscles and the cuteness of him holding his child.

It's been way too long since I've been on a date. For the first time since dad died, I feel like doing something other than going home, eating a shitty microwave meal and watching mindless TV to have noise in the house.

Before dad got sick, I had my own apartment. There was no question of me giving the place up and moving home to take care of him. Initially, he'd hated feeling like I was giving something up, but Dad was the most important person in my life, there was no way I was going to let him deal with his diagnosis alone. He was no burden to me.

When we found out why he'd not been feeling himself, it was the first time I ever saw my dad scared. He masked it, but I knew him too well. He feared dying. Who wouldn't? But he feared leaving me alone more. My whole life we'd been a team, the two of us had been there for one another through everything, good and bad.

The doctors told us the treatment could prolong his life. They were liars. His deterioration was so fast in fact, it felt like I'd been cheated. He was stolen from me within two months. Someone so full of love shouldn't be taken from the world when there are so many other people deserving of it.

Uncharitable thoughts aren't usually something I'm capable of, but he was my dad.

He wouldn't want me to drown in grief. It's time to do something I've been putting off. I need to be around people. I can already hear Dana's voice in my head when I call to say its time for that girl's night she's been trying to drag me to.

Parking the car besides Jesse's broken down one, I call my best friend.

"Taylor, I was just thinking about you."

"In what way?"

"In a *I haven's spoken to my bestie in two days* kind of way. Are you okay? Where are you?"

"Take a breath Dana. I'm good," I laugh. "I'm in work, well outside of work." I explain what happened, without going into detail about Jesse's private business.

"He does sound hot."

"That's what you got from the conversation."

"You literally said he was topless, tattooed, grumpy and good looking."

"I never."

"You did," she tells me. "Why are the hot ones always so irritating?"

"It's not like I'm going to see him again. Anyway, that wasn't why I was calling."

"Are you doing okay?" her tone changes. I'm not going to get defensive about it. Dana is one of the few I can be real in front of. I've cried many tears on her the past few months.

"Yes, I swear. Some days are easier than others but I'm good. In fact, I was gonna suggest we go out tonight."

"For real?"

"Yeah. Nothing crazy, a few drinks, maybe something to eat?"

Dana squeals. We've only been friends since college where I went into nursing while she did marketing. It feels like I've known her forever we click so well. Dad loved her too, and she loved him right back. She's the closest thing I have to a sibling, someone who knew dad and sees how hard this is hitting me.

"I know just the place. There is this guy-"

"Every single time, you start out with something about a guy."

"This one is hot guy goals though."

"Never heard that before."

"But we can totally have a quiet night if that is what you want."

Quiet nights are all I seem to have lately. It might be fun to watch Dana flirt around a new guy. "No, I wouldn't deprive you of your chance with the hot guy."

"If my wing woman needs more time, I'm good with that."

"What time and where?"

"I'll pick you up at eight."

It's a good job, it's Friday and I don't have to work tomorrow. Something tells me this is going to be a night to remember.

Chapter Four

Nero

"Are you out of your fucking mind?"

"I wasn't expecting my car to break down. You really didn't need to be that rude."

"She saw Oscar." I wave my hands in the air.

"And has no idea who you or Oscar are. If anything, you made it weird by telling her to forget what she saw. You realize that will make her wonder more than if you'd thanked her for helping me."

He's right. Of course he is. But I will never admit that. When I saw her following Jesse up to the house, my first thought was panic. Why the hell was a nurse coming back with him? What happened at the appointment to make him need a nurse escorting him here?

He was late getting back, and his phone was busy every time I called. Rebel had been texting about when I was going to get to the clubhouse too. He knew I was busy this morning with Oscar but he couldn't explain that to the others, being one of the few people who know he exists.

The nurse thing made my heart hammer in my chest. Then I noticed the grocery bags. And the fact Jesse arrived in her car and not his. And who the hell walks into a stranger's house like that?

And also, fuck, she is beautiful. Like, stop you in your tracks gorgeous, with hair the color of corn in a meadow, stunning gray eyes and the kind of body you want to feel yourself pressed up against, preferably naked, with your cock buried inside her.

Shit, now I'm about to sport a fucking erection when I'm mad as hell.

"What happened at the appointment?" I ask, changing the subject. I've got to get to the clubhouse, but I need to know he's okay. We can argue about bringing strangers here later.

He is right, she has no clue who I am, or any reason to spread the word that there is a kid here, at least to anyone who matters.

"Everything is fine. All my levels are good, nothing untoward going on."

"What about..." How do I ask this question?

"You'll be pleased to hear Taylor says its unlikely anything medical is causing it. She even queried if I'm attracted to my partner."

"You fucking with me? She asked you that?" I wave my arm at the front door.

"It was a logical question," he looks away, his cheeks flushing

Damn, this is hard for him to talk about. And I'm being a self-righteous prick, worrying about me instead of him. Jesse is always there for me, I have to step up now, even if I am in a hurry and the club comes first. Being supportive is what I should be doing.

"I thought you'd be happy, you hate James."

"I never said that."

He scoffs and deposits more groceries on the counter. We really need to talk about what is going on. The more I think about it, the more I wonder if he is avoiding something by spending all his time here, with Oscar.

"You don't have to open your mouth, Noah. You have subtitles written all over your face."

Can't even argue with that. With everything except the club, I make my feelings known. Jesse continues putting away groceries as I grab a T-shirt from the clean laundry pile and pull it on. It makes me remember how Taylor kept staring at me. She might have thought she was being sneaky, but she kept looking at my chest, and lower. Bet she hates herself for that.

Shrugging on my cut, I glance at Oscar to make sure he is okay. I fucking hate leaving him again but there is no other way I can deal with this situation.

"We can talk about this later. Or never," Jesse rounds the counter and looks at Oscar. "Have you given him lunch?"

"Yeah, he probably didn't need the snack, but you know he's a gingerbread junkie," I smile for the first time since he came home.

"The tow company is going to the clinic for my car so I might need a ride there to get the car back."

"I'll send someone for it," I say, heading over to say goodbye to my son, kissing the top of his head. He gives me a toothy grin and shoves a soggy gingerbread into his mouth.

We say nothing more, but Jesse gives me a knowing look. He won't be expecting an apology. I should give one anyway, I was out of line but I'm still stewing on the implications of that nurse seeing Oscar. And me if I'm honest. Why it's bothering me so much is a string I don't want to tug on.

So why on the ride over to Locust Point, do I keep thinking about her, wondering what it would be like to peel that nurse's uniform off of her?

All thoughts of the sexy nurse leave my head when I get to the clubhouse. Rebel is waiting and we go straight upstairs to the room where we hold Church. There aren't many rooms in the building, most of it is open plan.

The only thing up here is the large room that holds all of my officers when we need to meet. There are two bedrooms that are used mostly for the brothers who stay here so the clubhouse isn't empty. Or when someone wants to go fuck a club girl.

No one has been up here the past few nights. After Phoenix, my half brother caught his mom in here with one of the members and a bag of fucking cocaine, I'd barred anyone from using them for anything other than guard duty. It won't last long but I was pissed as hell.

We might move drugs and other illegal contraband, but I don't want it touching this place. It's ironic that I help people shift drugs all over the state, but won't let my men use it here.

If I had my way, no one would do it on their own time either, but I'm no one's keeper. Unless they fuck up because of it. Like Grim did, even worse, taking Phoenix's mom upstairs to fuck *while* doing it.

This has been my life from the moment I signed on as a prospect, following in my dad's footsteps. If all I can do is keep it out of the local community, I'm going to make damn sure no one in my club is using it.

That whole incident fucked up my relationship with Phoenix. He's asked me more than once to keep his mom away but I've dropped the ball because of all the other shit I've been dealing with. Phoenix is yet to answer any calls I've made to him for days.

Rebel closes the door behind us and goes to the table, dropping his lanky frame into the chair that the VP has always occupied. He's a good man, methodical thinking, cool in a crisis and someone I know I can rely on, no matter what. We were friends before we became officers together. That doesn't mean we slack in our roles.

He taps his finger against the table as I take my seat. This has been a long time coming. It's going to be impossible to blow him off again.

"I've kept everyone in line, but questions are being asked," he says.

"What have you told them?"

He shrugs. "Can't answer what I don't know."

He's right. I've kept this close to my chest for years. Rebel knows I am protective of Phoenix and will do anything to make sure the shit here doesn't touch my half-brother. What I've kept from Phoenix over the years doesn't even touch the surface of what he thinks is going on.

My mother namely. She's a fucking psycho when it comes to Phoenix. We share a father, different moms. Mine was his Old Lady, Kate was a club whore. It goes on, the majority of the guys here make use of the women that hang around.

Dad was notorious for it. Mom let it slide, until he knocked one of them up. The stupid bastard accidentally shot himself eleven years ago when he was drunk and cleaning a gun. He left a hell of a fucking mess behind when he did. And I've been cleaning up mom's messes ever since.

The worst time was when she put Kate in the hospital after beating the shit out of her and stabbing her in the leg. Phoenix blames me for his mom still coming around the club. After the whole drug fiasco, I can't blame him for avoiding me.

Kate is upstate at a rehab place now. I've offered to pay, but he's shut me out.

“Last night was a fuck up and rightfully so, people are asking why Dutton is nothing but broken teeth and old shoes.”

My lip curls in distaste at that visual. Pigs will eat anything. Except teeth apparently.

Might as well be blunt. “He murdered Ghost’s sister fifteen years ago.”

Rebel stares at me in silence for a few seconds, then he swears under his breath.

“If we didn’t do it, he was going to.”

“As was his right, don’t you think?” Rebel asks. He’s pissed. On both counts, finding out what Dutton did, and that we had to take him out when he could have potentially been useful.

Rebel’s sister works at the bar next door. Raven grew up in the club like Rebel. Like with other women, she’s not a member, but she is such a fixture around here that no one bothers when she gets into shit.

She is feisty as fuck and has had a few run-ins with the brothers but it’s more entertaining than annoying. Rebel keeps her in line if she goes too far, so I don’t worry. He's a protective bastard when it comes to Raven, hearing about Ghost’s sister makes him rethink the annoyance.

He’d tear apart anyone who hurt his sister with his bare hands.

“Ghost isn’t going to be an issue anymore. I've released him from the club.”

His brow lifts. “You need him.”

“He never was a true member.”

“Which is also something you’ve never fully explained.”

“Is there any point?”

He leans back. “Are you kicking him lose so you don’t have to explain what he did for you over the years?”

A smile curls my lips. Rebel shakes his head.

“What about the other idiot you were following that led us to Dutton?” he asks.

“He was a go between, he doesn’t know what the fuck is going on. Nashville scared the piss out of him last night. He’s being encouraged to move out of the apartment block.”

“After you left, I managed to get something out of him.” He ignores my glare and I let it go. “I’ve put feelers out about the name he gave us.”

“And?”

“Nothing, yet.” He rubs a hand across his jaw. "Blaze is working on it."

"We can figure it out."

After a long hard look, he gets up. "Stryker needs a word. Shall I send him up?"

"Gimme ten minutes, I've got some calls to make."

Rebel nods and leaves.

Someone is messing in Blackhawk Disciples business. For now, it's nothing too serious, but it has the potential to go bad. I need to stop it before it does. So far, we've struggled to figure out who is undermining us.

They're starting out small, but they've approached one of our business partners to offer them a *better* deal.

What my buyer doesn't realize is, the cut in prices is for a reason. It will eventually bite them in the ass. Either with subpar product, or bad protection. Rather than try to convince them I'm right, I'm going after the assholes trying to take business from me.

Closing my eyes I take a few moments to center myself.

Stryker is the club's Reaper. He will have been the one to run Dutton up to the Farm last night. He's quiet, keeps to himself, doesn't ask many questions. Fuck knows what he wants.

I check my phone and go to the chat with Phoenix. He's still left me on read. Fuck, that has got to change, and soon.

A text comes in before I can put the phone away. It's Jesse, letting me know his car has been fixed and is in the parking lot at the clinic.

Jesse: If you want to keep your identity a secret you better not send someone in a cut

Nero: Don't be a little bitch, it doesn't suit you

Jesse: Just following the rules

Nero: How is he?

Jesse: Changing the subject. Now who's the bitch...

Jesse: He's fine

He won't say anything more. Even though our phones are encrypted, thanks to Blaze my tech guy, we never discuss Oscar by name. I don't know what I would do without him helping me out right now.

Part of me wants to text back telling him we need a serious talk. I mean, he's the CEO of an international finance company, and he's hanging out with a two-year-old.

Whether he wants to hear it or not, I'm still worried about this latest visit to the diabetes clinic.

One thing is for sure, he's right about not showing up there with a huge identifier as to who we are.

I can send a Prospect. It's what I should do...

Nero: I'll sort it

From the buzzing I know he's replied and sent another two texts for good measure. I ignore them all and head downstairs. Stryker is leaning against the wall in the rec area next to the TV that is almost as large as the wall it's hanging on.

I don't know how Blaze got it, and I don't want to know but it entertains the guys and keeps things quiet here. They want to get rowdy, they go to the bar next door. I lift my chin at Stryker and head for the door. He follows me without a word, or even a microscopic change in his facial structure.

Rebel is leaning over his sister talking quietly. He spots me heading out, but I wave it off. Raven gives me a look that makes her brother bitch at her until she looks away. I'd never go there. Raven is beautiful, with her dark hair and eyes, but she is trouble I can do without.

Hell, the one and only time I messed around with one of the guy's sisters, I got her pregnant.

She said it was a faulty condom. It wasn't a way to control me or get something from me. It was a genuine mistake on both our parts, one with lifelong repercussions forcing us to remain attached.

Sheridan doesn't want anything from me. She only wants what Oscar is rightfully owed, a dad, and financial support.

"We need a cage," I tell Stryker. "I've got to do a pickup."

Stryker nods. He's a quiet guy, keeps to himself mostly. Except when he's fighting. He's been making his way up the ranks in an underground statewide cage fighting circuit. He's good enough to go professional and is a star attraction when he does fight, but he will never do it. To him, the fighting is a release, a way to pass time and get out all the rage bottled up inside of him.

I'm not worried he's going to leave the club anytime soon. Stryker is as loyal as they come. I'm only mildly concerned he wants to talk. He disappears back inside to find the keys to one of the cars we keep around when taking the bikes isn't possible.

When he comes back, we head to the warehouse next to the bar and get into a black soft top jeep that officially belongs to Beast. We share all the cages, the name we give cars amongst the MC, because that is exactly what it feels like when you're riding around in one, instead of on a bike.

The clinic isn't too far from my house in Fairmount, but it takes about twenty minutes to get there from the clubhouse. Plenty of time for Stryker to tell me why he needed to talk. I let him get to it in his own time, my mind occupied with my own thoughts.

What exactly am I doing? Taylor isn't going to be thrilled to see me. That kind of makes me feel better about doing this. She's a firecracker for sure. Not even my most menacing glare or my shitty behavior stopped her from speaking her mind and calling me out. It was in defense of Jesse, so I can let it pass. Maybe.

We're halfway there when Stryker finally speaks.

"At my fight last night, got talking to one of the other fighters. He was pissed because he found out his opponent threw the match for some guy betting on the fight."

"That's fucked up," I shake my head.

Not because I don't believe him, but because throwing a fight is a bullshit move. Stryker takes it seriously and cheating doesn't sit right with him. From the sound of it, the other guy didn't appreciate it either, even though he won because of it.

"This what you need to talk to me about, you want to do something about the betting situation?"

"No, I've got that shit handled. It's what he overheard about who wanted him to take the deal. And who came to him and made it."

We come to a set of lights and Stryker slows to a stop.

"It took everything I had not to go find him and rip his head off. It's not my place to make that choice without your say so."

The clinic is across the intersection. Jesse's car is sitting in the lot waiting for me to pick it up. He looks over toward the clinic too, I had to tell him the destination given he was driving.

This isn't the place to hear what Stryker has to say. I need to hear it, regardless.

"Who?" I ask, my jaw clenched as I stare through the windshield.

"Chains."

For half a second, I consider putting a fist through the glove compartment, but I reign myself in and don't take my eyes off Jesse's clinic.

"And the person he is working for?"

"Storm."

For a man of so few words, everything he said is pretty fucking impactful. Storm is an ex-Disciple who was stripped of his patch. There is a whole lot of history there but he's remained quiet this long, I figured there was no animosity.

Now it's all starting to make sense. And I didn't even need Ray Dutton to get me there.

"What do you want me to do?" Stryker asks. The light turns green.

"Pull into the lot," I say, jaw tight. "You told anyone else?"

Stryker shakes his head as he turns into the lot as I asked.

"Keep it that way. For now."

He nods, not happy, but he'll do as he's told. There are many reasons why this pisses him off and I'm glad to see he feels that way, and has brought this to me. His loyalty is to the patch, not blood.

"And my cousin?" He turns to me as he pulls the car to a stop. His eyes are flashing dangerously. It's the way he looks right before he enters the ring. Like he's ready to tear his opponent apart.

"I'll figure that out."

Stryker nods. He's done with talking. Fuck. One of our own is working with an ex-member. And I'm not sure how deep it runs.

I get out of the car but keep the door open as I slip off my cut. Stryker's eyes widen. That is more animated than he was during his confession his family member may be a rat. He watches me fold it and set it on the seat.

"Take that to my house, leave it with Jesse."

Another head nod, his Adam apple bobs as he swallows. It should be funny, that me taking off my cut affects him so badly. But I see something else in the way he's looking at me. Honor. That I'm trusting him with this. Stryker knows having a family member screw over the club could see his standing tarnished. Me doing this, gives him validation of his place.

It's all so fucking messed up. I feel naked as hell without it as Stryker drives away to carry out my order. I fire a text to Jesse letting him know something is being dropped off, then look up at the clinic.

My eyes are immediately drawn to the woman standing by the entrance. She is sweeping her hair away from her neck, her face momentarily tipped towards the sunlight. No longer in her scrubs, she's changed into a pair of tight, high-waisted jeans and a blue short-sleeved shirt which is tucked in at the waist.

Fuck me.

Yeah, that is probably not what she is going to want to hear coming out of my mouth. Which is watering as I take her in. The scrubs hid a lot. Damn, those tits would look so much better with my inked hands wrapped around them.

She starts walking, tossing a large bag over her shoulder but her steps falter when she sees me. Her lips part slightly and even though we're standing far apart from one another, I sense the intake of breath as she comes to a stop.

We stare at each other, and I fight the urge to smirk. She has no such compunction. Her face morphs into an angry scowl, her lips are full and the color of ripe, juicy cherries. Wonder if that is what she tastes like too?

Yeah, despite the shit storm brewing within the Disciples, that scowl on her gorgeous face is all I can fucking see right now.

Chapter Five

Taylor

Leaving the clinic, my heart feels a little less heavy, despite the strange interaction earlier today. Shannon is letting me go back on rotation next week, not quite a full clinic, but it's better than sitting behind a desk or seeing two patients a day.

I'm not going to lose it, or be unable to cope with seeing patients. Watching the person you love most in the world waste away to cancer is nothing like what we do here.

It's not like diabetes doesn't come with its own complications but the people who come to see us have their treatment well under control.

Tonight is going to be a big night for my next step in the grieving process, I guess. I'm going to take my time getting ready for the night out with Dana wherever she is about to take me. I will have fun no matter what.

The company who came to look at Jesse's car didn't take it away, they fixed it right in the lot. I called Jesse a half hour ago to let him know, he paid over the phone and said he'd be here as fast as he could to take the keys. I could have left them inside but chose to wait for him instead.

Except it's not Jesse standing beside the car. My steps falter and I stop and stare at him across the lot. Why did Jesse not tell me it was *him* coming to get the car? And why is he staring at me as if his eyes are eating me alive?

He moves first and starts toward me. As he draws closer, all the blood in my body rushes south and a not so unfamiliar heat begins to pulse between my legs. I fight it. I'm *not* getting turned on by watching this man walk. My brain helpfully reminds me I've seen him without his shirt, and I've been starved of attention from the opposite sex for a long time.

Before dad got ill, I'd been going through a prolonged dry spell. This reaction is making me equal parts hot, and irritated as hell that I'm letting him get to me. Which is why the words that fall out of my mouth are less than polite.

"What the hell are you doing here?"

One perfectly curved eyebrow lifts, and another thump pulses, my pelvic muscles waking up.

"I thought that was obvious." He answers, coming to a stop closer than I would like.

I resist the urge to step back. Man, he's tall, and he smells good. Don't forget he's an ass. He spoke to you like you were a piece of shit on his shoe earlier. Treacherous hormones can go screw themselves.

"Where is Jesse?"

"The car needs collecting. I'm here to pick it up."

"Manners cost nothing you know," I say, lifting my chin. I'm not afraid of this guy.

"I could say the same thing to you," he tilts his head.

"Meaning? I'm not the one being rude."

"What the hell are you doing here?" He repeats my words back to me, sounding far too smug for my liking.

My cheeks flush because he's right. I was rude. But he started it. Oh god, now I'm thinking like a petulant five-year-old. I can be the bigger person here. Said the medium-sized woman to the gigantic man.

"I was expecting Jesse."

"Well, you got me." He shoves a hand in his pocket.

"Do you always boss Jesse around?" I ask before my brain tells me it's a bad idea.

He huffs out a laugh, there is no amusement to it whatsoever. It makes me mad again.

"What exactly is it that you think is going on between me and Jesse?"

My mouth opens and closes. I'd thought a lot about what Jesse said as I drove back to the clinic. I still think he was lying about Noah being his unrequited crush. Who can blame him?

"You clued in yet?" His eyes drop to my lips, then back to my eyes. "Men don't do it for me, sweetheart."

"I'm not your sweetheart," I say automatically. "That is no excuse to talk to him the way you did."

"Why do you care so much?"

"Because he is a nice guy and you... aren't."

"Again, you say I'm the one with no manners."

Well, this is getting us nowhere. "Okay, fine. I'll apologize for being rude, so long as you do."

"You want me to say sorry? For what?"

My lips pinch together. He's trying to antagonize me. I'm done with that. "Here." I grab the keys from my purse and thrust them at him.

"I *appreciate* that." He annunciates the word. Like an ass.

I drop them into his outstretched hand, making sure to avoid touching him. I've got a feeling that would be my undoing right now. Not quite sure if it would be in a good or a bad way.

He got close enough to feel the heat coming from his body, smell the clean-soap scent of his skin. I'm really glad I freshened up and changed before heading out. I'm usually in my scrubs after a long, hard day and probably not smelling my best.

Why do I care?

I expect him to thank me or say something. Instead, he looks me up and down again, then turns and goes to the car. What a damn jerk. Seriously. When he gets to the driver's side he looks at me over the roof of the car.

"Have the day you deserve, sweetheart."

It's difficult, but I keep the anger off my face and clench my fist to prevent giving him my middle finger. He doesn't deserve any kind of reaction. This morning, he could maybe be forgiven for his attitude, I did invite myself into his house without asking. Still rude, but okay I can let that go.

Taking it further when he shows up to collect a car I've done them a favor over... Hell no. I wish I was more than Jesse's nurse right now, because I would tell him to run as far and as fast away from that man as he can.

Fuming both at him and myself for letting him get to me, I stomp to my car and do not watch him driving away.

After a meal, shower and quick change of outfit, I stand in front of the mirror in my childhood bedroom and stare at my reflection. I've gone with jeans and a sleeveless black shimmery top. It's not over the top glamorous but enough to make me feel like I've made an effort.

Dana arrives after eight.

"If you ever show up on time, I think I'll have a coronary."

She rolls her eyes. "I don't even know why you're surprised," she tugs on my braid. "You look very cute by the way. Are you ready for a fun night?" She links my arm and drags me to the mirror in the hallway, stopping so we're both facing it, and smiles at me in the reflection.

"I'm ready," I tell her, when she stares expectantly, waiting for my reply.

"Then let's go have some fun." Her smile is genuine, but she can't hide the concern or sadness behind her eyes.

"We will," I take her hand and give it a squeeze. "So long as you tell me where we're going."

"Oh, well, that is a surprise."

She drags me to the front door, her eyes pausing on a photograph of me and dad when I was around fifteen. We don't dwell and head outside where a cab is idling at the sidewalk.

Dana keeps fiddling with her earring, a telltale sign she is excited but nervous. And if she is displaying this side of her, then this is about the guy.

"Who is he?"

Her lips twist into a coy smile. "He came into the bar a few times. He was hot and closed off, you know, just my type."

"Dana."

"He could be my one true love, Tay."

"I've heard that before," I grin at her. There is no point in talking her out of this. I literally have heard this more times than I can count.

The drive takes a while, and I watch the surroundings change to the more affluent area of Locust Point. We never go this far for a night out. What on earth is she getting us into? That soon becomes apparent when we pull up at a bar that has a lot of motorcycles out front.

My head snaps to her as the cab stops.

"Before you get mad, it's a nice place. The woman who runs it is cool and although there are bikers here, she keeps them in line. I promise, you're safe here. Raven would kick anyone's ass if they bother us. Beyond how we want to be bothered at least."

Well, we're here now. We get out of the cab and I glance around. It's not exactly an industrial area but there are a couple of warehouse-style buildings next to the bar. It is well lit and there are houses further back, as well as a church.

It's the bikers I'm not so sure about.

We head over, passing by rows of motorcycles and a few cars and step inside the bar. I won't lie, I was expecting some dive with sawdust on the floor, sweat dripping down the walls and gangs of old men with long beards and leather jackets.

That isn't what greets me. This place is nice, modern, with oak wood floors, dark but stylishly decorated with booths. It has tall tables and stools and a long bar with a mirrored wall behind it.

There are two women behind the bar serving people, wearing t-shirts with the name of the bar. The tables are occupied by a mixture of people. Yes, there are bikers, who are obvious by their leather vests but they're all in one corner chatting and laughing.

The place is packed, but the music isn't loud, there is an air of people having a good time about it and I instantly relax. Dana was right. A gorgeous woman with tattoo sleeves, sleek black hair, wearing a deep red sleeveless dress with a dangerously low V-neck spots Dana and holds up a hand waving her over. Her look is as stylish as the bar, not slutty.

Instantly I hate myself for thinking that. We make our way through the tables to the bar and the woman comes out and gives Dana a hug. We're introduced, and she gives me a friendly smile and wave. There is a moment where she watches me though, gauging how I'm going to react.

I choose not comment on the bar at all and that seems to satisfy her.

“What are we drinking tonight ladies?”

“Cocktails,” Dana laughs. “Lots of cocktails.”

Raven smirks and hands us both menus. Menus. Jesus, I really am a judgmental ass. She takes us to a table close to the bar but near the back of the room so we won’t be bothered. It’s probably the best table in the whole place.

“You can relax,” Dana tells me.

“Let’s pretend I didn’t have preconceived ideas about this place and move on.”

She laughs and looks at her menu. We settle on what we want and Dana gives our order to one of the staff who says she will be right back. Raven is chatting with a few people at the bar, laughing and pouring drinks.

I can’t help but stare at her tattoos. They are beautiful, like she is. But they remind me of someone else. Someone I’ve been trying really damn hard not to think about. The server returns with our cocktails, setting down napkins first and tells us to give her a shout when we’re ready for more.

Dana sips through her straw and lets out a sigh of pleasure. “Try it,” she encourages. “They’re orgasmic.”

“Well, that’s an endorsement. And probably the only orgasm I’m getting any time soon.”

Dana laughs. We chat a bit about work, and I tell her that it wasn’t so bad. In fact, I’m happy to be back because it means I get back to some form of normalcy.

“Don’t put pressure on yourself,” she touches my arm. “Just let things happen, don’t shy away and don’t throw yourself at things either.”

“So go with the flow,” I sip my cocktail. “Got it.”

We both laugh. We’re not too far from the men in leather vests and I try to see what it says on the back but no one is sitting the right way. Dana catches me looking.

“They’re called the Blackhawk Disciples. And yes, they’re a biker gang but Raven grew up around them and said they’re pussycats.”

“If you believe that,” I give her a side-eyed look.

“Yeah well, a little danger never hurt anyone.”

“Speaking of, who is this guy you’re hot for. Is he one of them?”

She tries to look demure as she smiles. “Maybe.”

"Where is he?"

"Not here yet," she pouts. "But he will be, he comes here but sometimes it's late."

"Mhm," I drink some more of my cocktail. It's really good, you can hardly taste the alcohol which is what makes it dangerous. I don't have anywhere I need to be tomorrow so when we finish our first, we call for another which Raven drops off promptly. She winks at us before sashaying away.

"She's my hero," Dana watches after her. "I want to be her."

"There is nothing wrong with who you are," I poke her arm. "You're beautiful, funny, talented and the best friend a girl could ask for."

"Aw," she leans into me for a second. Then eyes my drink. "Maybe you need something a little less... loaded," she laughs.

"I am not drunk." Not yet, but I do feel a little lighter.

This was definitely a good idea. I'm even coming around to the venue. Only thing that remains to be seen, is this guy Dana is drooling over. If he ever gets here.

Chapter Six

Nero

DOWNSTAIRS IS QUIET. I sent those who were hanging around over to the bar, because what we need to discuss here cannot be overheard by anyone except my council. Stryker's bombshell from earlier today has been on repeat inside my head.

A fucking traitor. I got complacent, thinking Storm was in the past. Kept an eye on him for a while to be sure but after three years, I let it go, taking Ghost off his tail. Fuck, I wish I could call Ghost right now to pick that back up.

The other thing that keeps plaguing my thoughts, and one I'm fighting with everything I have, is Cherry.

Jesus, I've even given her a fucking nickname. Her swollen cherry red lips keep popping into my head at the most inopportune moments. I've spent far too long imagining them, wrapped around my cock preferably, smearing cherry red lipstick all over me.

I push her from my mind. She is not my concern. If anything, I need to steer clear of her, I'm the one who told her to forget we ever met after all.

We're on Disciples turf here, that is what I need to focus on. Not the sexy, spitfire nurse who's lips I want to devour to see if they taste as good as I imagine. Cherries have always been a weakness.

Every one of my officers is in the room. Rebel got Raven to give him a couple of bottles of her best whisky from the bar. She'd made him pay for them before she handed them over. He's been grumbling about it since he got in here.

I filled him in on what this was about before I gathered everyone here. Rebel understood we're going to need it.

Stryker has been quiet. He's a man of few words as it is, but the news he brought to me has rendered him mute. When you find out family is not only fucking you over, but everything you hold dear, it will do that to you.

When I dropped Jesse's car at home and grabbed my cut, he said Stryker didn't say a word, handed over the cut and walked away. He'd also quizzed me about my trip to the clinic and the fact I even took off my cut but I waved him off. It's unexplainable.

I look around at my men, we've talked about other business and everyone has had a couple of drinks. But now it's time to get down to the real problem. Stryker is standing apart from us, leaning against the wall holding his glass. It's not disrespect, he often stands when we're holding Church, but tonight it's different. I'm not having him feel separated and catch his attention.

"Take your seat."

He hesitates for a beat, then pushes off the wall and sits beside Blaze, our club secretary, clasping his hands on the table. His knuckles are bruised and cut after his last fight. The one where he learned what his cousin is doing.

He knew this moment would come the minute he told me what he found out. The brothers won't judge him, but his shoulders are tense, anyway.

Everyone listens as I explain, not making Stryker even more uncomfortable by asking him to repeat it.

The men around the table became my council within days of me starting my presidency. I handpicked them all because I trust them. Knowing there is a traitor in our ranks has them in varying degrees of annoyance. Rebel shows the least reaction, his questions will come after everyone has gone.

Whereas Beast our Tail Gunner is visibly upset, he's been close to Chains for years.

"Are you sure?" he asks, leaning forward to see Stryker.

"Would I make this up?" he asks without raising his head.

"We need to kick him out, after we kick his fucking ass," Fury leans back in his chair, resting one elbow on the arm rest, his fist clenched.

After I let them have their say, they all look at me. "I appreciate you are all pissed about this. I am too. Chains has been with us for a long time. He's been a friend, a brother and he's family," I nod towards Stryker, but he still has his head down. "You all know we've been looking for answers about who is coming at us and this is a solid lead. Right now, that is all it is."

Stryker's head comes up, his expression is unreadable to most. It's not that I don't trust his intel, we need to see it firsthand and not believe a man at a cage fight who was pissed about what happened to him. I explain that to them all and more discussions ensue about the best course of action.

"There is merit to what we have learned," I say when they've all quietened down. "But we are going to look into this ourselves."

"Prez, Storm is a fucking traitor who has held a grudge from the moment we kicked him out. You know he is capable of this shit."

"I've heard what everyone has had to say," I tell Fury.

As the club's enforcer, it often falls to him to handle situations like this. He was the one who burned Storm's patch tattoo off his arm before we kicked him out.

"Nashville," I look to my sergeant-at-arms. "Get close to Chains, watch him, try to feel him out. Stryker, be yourself, don't change your habits but keep your ear to the ground at the ring. Beast, I know your friends with Chains, are you going to be able to be around him and not give anything away?"

"If he's a fucking traitor like Storm, he is no friend to me, Prez," he shakes his head and his face hardens. "I know what I need to do."

"Good. Blaze, find out everything you can about where he's been, who he's talking to, texts, emails, anything you can find. Storm too. I want to know everyone he has spoken to, worked with, fucked, right down to the tiniest detail over the last three years."

I warn everyone else to do what they can and to keep this information behind these doors. If Chains is a traitor, and Storm thinks he can come after this MC, I intend to make sure he never sees us coming.

Once everyone is dismissed and filed out, Rebel gets up from his seat. Nashville glances back, sees us standing together and closes the door behind him.

"Stryker wouldn't turn on his cousin if he didn't believe it."

"I know," I rub a hand over my head. Rebel is the only one who gets to see the less authoritative side of me. It's why he is my VP.

"You're probably doing the right thing," he says.

"Probably?" I give him a look.

His smile is grim. "We can't drag our heels on this. If he is what Stryker thinks he is, letting him stay here is going to look bad."

"Getting as much information out of him while he still thinks he's safe is more important than how it looks. The others will see that."

"You have doubts?" Rebel reads me with ease.

I think on it for a moment, then shake my head. "No, you're right, Stryker wouldn't have come to me if he didn't believe it of his own family. Make sure Blaze works fast on finding connections. Keep an eye on Fury, he didn't take Storm's departure well and we both know he can let his emotions get the better of him."

Rebel snorts. "That's one way to put it."

Storm was in the hospital for three weeks after Fury finished with him.

"I thought it was bad before," I grab my phone and push it into my pocket. "If this is coming from within, it is going to get so much worse."

Rebel doesn't answer. He knows what I mean. If we have one traitor, there may be more.

"What are you going to do now?" Rebel asks.

He doesn't mean about this, he means in general. He's probably expecting me to go home but the way I'm feeling right now, I can't take this back to the house. Jesse will have already put Oscar to bed so all I would do is go home and brood.

"It's been a fucking week," I blow out a heavy sigh. "Let's go next door."

His smile says he is down with that idea. It is not off my mind, but having a few drinks and trying to put it out of my mind for a few hours is the best thing I can do right now.

We enter the bar through the back entrance, which is connected by a short hallway I had built a couple of years ago. Only my officers use it and Raven because it leads to her bar and she demanded access.

The place is busy tonight, it's Friday after all. A bunch of brothers are gathered at a table near where we enter, some are at the bar and I spot Raven chatting with a few of the locals who are regulars here. It's not usually my scene but if it can take me out of my head for a while, then I'll deal with it.

Raven spots me and her brother, says something to the girl behind the bar, who passes over a bottle and two glasses, then she comes over.

"Wasn't expecting to see you in here tonight."

Rebel rolls his eyes. "It's our bar."

"Fuck you, douchebag. It's mine."

This is an old argument. Truth is the bar does belong to the club, for a lot of years. When Raven took it over, she turned the place around, it became less of a biker hangout and more a part of the neighborhood, which is what I've always wanted for the club. It may not be her name on the deed, but as far as I'm concerned, the place is hers.

I'm not getting between the two of them and their petty squabbles, I know better.

"Thanks," I take the bottle and glasses and turn around.

"Oh, I put someone else at your usual table. I didn't know you were going to come in tonight."

"What the fuck did you do that for?" Rebel snaps.

"It's no big deal," I motion to empty stools at the bar.

"I can ask them to move," Raven says. "But I don't want to."

"Jesus," Rebel shakes his head.

"It's fine, I just want a couple of drinks and to not be bothered," I turn again and glance at our table and stop in my tracks.

It's Cherry...

My first instinct is to run my eyes over her, to feel like the fantasies I've been having all day have manifested her here. Then my suspicions grow. I haven't got to be a successful president by not trusting my gut.

Three times in one day, when shit is going down at my club. And now she's here at the club bar.

No, this is far too much of a coincidence.

I'm going to find out what the fuck she is doing in here.

Rebel sees the change in my body language and follows where I'm staring. He glances back at Raven then turns his back on her.

"What's wrong? Or should I say which one do you want?"

"I've seen her three times today."

His jovial mood changes instantly. "She's following you?"

Is she? Technically... She works at the clinic where Jesse is cared for. He said she was his nurse. I don't know how long she's been there. Has she been getting close to him for a reason? She barged her way into my house this morning and she saw Oscar, that could be put down to her helping him out, bringing in the groceries.

Then it was me who showed up at the clinic, not her coming to find me. But that could have been orchestrated too. It isn't only men who can betray and cheat. And using a woman to get closer to me, find out about my son is one way of doing it.

"Doubt it. Send Speedway to the house anyway, tell him not to go inside, only keep watch."

Speedway is Sheridan's brother and knows about Oscar. He isn't here tonight, and he lives near to my place.

Rebel takes out his phone to do as I ask.

As I watch, Taylor gets up from the chair and straightens out her top. She laughs at something the woman with her says, who is pointing towards the bathrooms. Taylor walks in that direction, she doesn't see me.

Or maybe she is making a point of not looking at me. Maybe she is going to tell someone where I am. I shove the bottle and glasses at Rebel and follow her.

No one is getting the drop on me, especially not her.

Chapter Seven

Taylor

Despite myself, I'm having a good time. The bar is great and although another group of bikers arrived a little while ago, it hasn't got rowdier. In fact, the atmosphere initially changed when they walked in from the back. Dana didn't even know there was a way in from there.

She eyed the new group and looked disappointed.

"What's wrong?"

"He's still not here," she chews on her lower lip. "That guy, there the mean looking one, he is usually with him."

"Mean looking one," I laugh.

Although taking the time to study them I'm not sure which one she is talking about, because they all look a little mean, no that's the wrong word. Tough. They all look tough. Like they could take on anyone and win.

"The one with his hair shaved at the sides, he's a little older than the rest of them."

"Maybe he's running late," I say with a sympathetic shrug. It's after ten already. I know it's Friday, and I haven't exactly been a party animal lately, but people come out after ten or eleven sometimes. "Where did you meet him, anyway?"

"At the Battleground."

"Dana," I set my drink down too fast, and it sloshes over the top. Good job Raven gives out napkins with her cocktails.

"What?" she looks away guiltily.

"You know that place is dangerous, and illegal," I hiss.

"But there are always so many nice things to look at."

"Only you could think illegal fighters are nice to look at. Who is taking you there? Is it Evan? He should know better."

"He likes it too. We're not there trolling for men, we like to watch the fights. And Stryker is one of the best."

"That's his name?"

"Mhm, he's in the club."

"This one. He's a biker *and* a cage fighter. Wow."

"When you see him you'll understand," she nudges my knee with hers. "He's really hot, and mysterious. He barely talks."

"So how do you know you like the guy?"

"It's called the getting to know you phase. He's in the zone at the Battleground but we caught each other's eye, we shared a moment."

My eyes narrow. "Dana, have you even spoken to this man?"

"Well, duh, that's why we're here."

I close my eyes and count to five. Then blow out a breath and smile at her. Life's too short, I know that better than anyone. I'm not going to yell at her or tell her she's being reckless. If she likes this guy, and she wants to see where things could go, I'm not going to stop her. But I will remind her to be careful.

She listens to my advice and nods while her smile beams brighter with each word.

"I knew I keep you around for a reason."

"Yeah, well, wait and see if he shows. And if he doesn't, screw him," I lift my glass, she does the same and we clink. "His loss."

"I'm not giving up yet," she pulls back her glass and downs what is left.

"I need the bathroom," I tell her.

Dana points them out to me and I get up and grab my purse. I don't have to ask Dana to watch my drink, she's already slotting a drink protector over the top.

She was spiked once when we were in college, luckily the guy who did it was too messed up to even remember who he'd done it too, but she ended up at the ER having her stomach pumped. Ever since then, no matter where we are, she uses that cover and does the same for me.

Following her directions I walk through a doorway and look for the bathroom sign, then head left, passing the men's room first. I can still hear the music and chatter from the bar and the lights are brighter back here, but the ladies room is round another corner. I haven't felt unsafe all night so I'm not all that concerned.

Until someone grabs my arm and spins me around, pushing my back against the wall. I open my mouth to scream then see *him.*

What the hell? The moment of recognition and slight relaxing of my body goes out the window when I see his expression. What is this guys problem? He was annoyed this morning, irritated but cocky this afternoon, now he looks like a maniac.

"Let me go," I try to pull my arm away and glare at him. "What the hell are you doing?"

"Why are you here?" he asks, leaning in close and putting his forearm up against the wall by my head.

"Let me go or I'll scream."

"Tell me why you're here," he repeats, but he releases my arm. He doesn't step back though, keeping me pressed up against the wall. He isn't touching me, but he might as well have his full weight against me the way he's making me feel right now.

"I'm having drinks with my friend," I rush out. Adrenalin is racing through my veins and my fight-or-flight response is kicking in. He may be Jesse's friend, but I don't know him and he has no damn right to put his hands on me. "This is a bar."

"It's my bar," he growls.

That's weird. I take a second to look down and notice he is wearing a leather vest too. There is a badge across his chest that says President. I'm not stupid, I've seen TV shows and movies about motorcycle clubs. President is a big deal. *Holy crap.*

"Are you following me? Who sent you?"

"Oh my god, are you insane?"

I finally get my wits about me and put my hands on his chest, pushing him back. He doesn't move much but does take a small step away. His arm is still by my head. I go to move around him but he sidesteps, stopping me.

"Why on earth would I follow you? I didn't even plan to go out tonight, my friend wanted to meet someone who comes here. I didn't know this was where we were going until we pulled up outside."

And why am I explaining this to him? Because he is scaring me. And this is the only way I can get myself out of the situation. That, or a knee to the balls. I go to move my leg but he moves out of the way.

"I wouldn't do that if I were you."

"You've cornered me in a dark hallway, you're practically pinning me to a wall and demanding to know if I'm following you. Do you know how fucking deranged that is. You're lucky I haven't already kneed you in the balls, you absolute ass."

I'm not usually one to curse but he's bringing it out in me. Although ass isn't exactly one of my finest insults. His brow lifts as he stares down at me. This man could do me serious harm and despite the bravado, I'm afraid.

He's breathing hard as his eyes flick back and forth on mine, some of the rage is lifting. His eyes lower to my mouth and his lips part. What the hell?

"Can you please step back?"

"Not until you answer some questions."

Someone comes around the hallway, and I look over his shoulder to call for help. It's another man in a leather vest, when he sees us, he goes back to the bar. I'm on my own here. Until Dana comes looking for me.

"Did someone ask you to come here tonight, to see if I was here?"

"No, I already told you. This is the first time I've been out for over five months. I came here with my friend. Why are you asking me this? I only met you for the first time this morning. I have no idea who you are, I didn't even know you were in this gang."

His lip kicks up on one side. Oh really? That's funny.

"So if I check your phone I wouldn't see anything about me."

"Full of yourself, huh?" I shake my head. "No. Aside from thinking you're a rude asshole who doesn't deserve a friend like Jesse, I haven't even thought about you."

"Liar."

I open my mouth to argue but the tone of his voice has changed.

"I saw the way you looked at me this morning."

"Like you're a piece of crap, glad you got that."

He smirks full on now, like he's enjoying himself. He's giving me whiplash. Suddenly he's stopped thinking I'm following him? Paranoid much. Jesus.

"Maybe you are here with a friend," he says, his arm moves off the wall but he reaches out to touch my hair. "Maybe she did choose this bar at random."

He's leaning in closer making my heart start to pound. Seriously? He's getting me hot, and not in a bad tempered kind of way. What the hell is wrong with me?

"And maybe," he goes on, moving even closer. "You didn't look at me like you wanted to climb all over me."

"As if," I breathe out.

"You're really bad at hiding your feelings, Cherry. It's written all over your face."

"Cherry? That isn't my name." Has he got me confused with someone else, is that what this is about?

"Your lips are the color of cherries," he says, his eyes dipping there again.

My lips squeeze and I swallow hard. My chest is heaving and I'm fighting really hard not to let his voice and his nearness get to me. This man grabbed me and scared the life out of me, accused me of something I haven't done...

So why is there an ache in my lower stomach, spreading between my legs?

"And ever since I saw you this morning, I've wondered if they taste the same."

He reaches up a hand and runs his thumb over my lower lip, tugging it down slightly. I'm caught in some kind of messed up trap here. I should be doing what I threatened him with. He deserves a knee to the balls at the very least. Or a slap. Or something.

And I really ought to push his hand away as it trails over my chin, neck and lower to my breastbone.

Too low. I reach up to grab his wrist before he can touch me anywhere else even if my nipples are beading and pushing against the fabric of my bra. There are all kinds of things going on in my underwear.

His eyes flare and he stares so deep into me, it's like he can read every dirty little thought my brain is flashing over.

"Maybe I'll get to find out some time," he says, his mouth a few inches from mine.

Not a chance. That is what I mean to say, but nothing comes out. He steps back, and it's like a puppet string has been cut, I slump back against the wall as he takes a few paces back.

"Don't do anything I wouldn't do," he says then turns and walks away.

A little whimper escapes me and I shake my head. Was that real? Did I really get turned on by a man threatening me? He thinks I'm following him?

Getting my wits about me I go to the bathroom, because despite all of that I really need to pee. When I come back to the bar, Dana is chatting with Raven. My eyes search the whole place but there is no sign of Noah. Dana looks up with a smile, but it falls when she sees my expression.

"Tay, is everything alright?"

"Fine. Did your man show?"

"Um, no. Raven said he isn't coming."

"Okay, thanks Raven, it's been fun meeting you. Can we go?" I look at Dana.

"Is everything alright?" Raven asks. "Did something happen?"

She works for him. This is his bar. She's one of them. I can't tell her what happened back there, he's the president of this motorcycle club, no one is going to take my side. I'm too freaked out to stay or explain. I promise them I'm fine, just tired and Dana agrees. Raven says they have a contract with a cab company and arranges for one to take us home.

Dana is worried but I do one of the worst things ever, I use my father as an excuse. She hugs me in the back of the cab and says she is proud of me for trying and even offers to spend the night, but I tell her I'm good.

I lock up the house as she leaves in the cab and walk through to the kitchen, taking out a bottle of vodka and pouring a shot. More alcohol is not what I need but my nerves are shot to hell.

My brain runs through everything he said to me and each interaction I've had with him today. I don't think the way he does, I can't come to the same conclusion he has that the few times we met today is anything other than coincidence.

He was so paranoid that I was at his house this morning and accusing me of following him tonight. Who does that? Then I remember his vest, the patch, who he really is. It makes me wonder if Jesse is a part of that lifestyle. It's really going to suck when I have to see him again, and that makes me sad.

Setting the alarm I head up to bed, stripping out of my clothes and washing off my make-up, I throw on some fluffy pajamas and get into bed. Sleep is a really long time coming and not because of all the alcohol I consumed.

There must be something wrong with me because I've gone beyond thinking about the bad stuff and am caught up on how he stared at my mouth. How he called me Cherry. And that sort of, kind of promise that he is going to taste my lips.

Chapter Eight

Nero

I PARK MY BIKE in the alley at the back of the Blackhawk Ink Tattoo shop. I understand he doesn't want me coming in the shop, but it still pisses me off. Unlike the bar, Ghost or Garrett as he asked me to call him when I arranged this meeting, does own this place now, it hasn't been under our ownership for almost seven years.

He kept the name because of the reputation it's built. That is down to Garrett and Phoenix, they're both phenomenal tattooists. Garrett has done a lot of my ink and usually does the club patch on any new members, he even has it on his own forearm.

Being kept waiting is not going to do him any favors. I'm leaning against the wall opposite the door when it opens. Garrett steps out and pulls it over. He lifts his chin in greeting.

"How's Phoenix?" I ask.

"He's coming around," he says, shoving his hands into his pockets.

We never were the kind to have heart to hearts. We knew what each of us wants from the other and the relationship never went much further than that.

"He's talked about calling."

That's good to hear. I hate fighting with him. I've looked out for him my whole life. I'm not here to make any more small talk.

"Dutton's dealt with."

Garrett's head comes up, his jaw tight, and he nods. He wanted to be the one to do it, to take his revenge but the man who was my Ghost isn't a violent person. He knows he owes me.

"I've got one more job."

It's on the tip of his tongue to protest but again he nods. "After that I'm out?"

I make him wait for a few moments. "Yeah. You were never really in to begin with."

"But when I say out, I mean out, completely, no favors, no contact, no tattoos."

"Shit, that's a bit excessive. You and my brother are the best artists in the state."

Garrett stares at me. I know he means patch tattoos. To be fair, I don't have plans for any new tattoos, anyway. And Phoenix won't be as hard as Garrett if I want one. I don't even need to come to the shop if it makes everyone more comfortable.

See, I can be a reasonable sonofabitch sometimes. I take an envelope out of my jacket pocket and hold it out to him. "I don't need surveillance. I want a full background check."

"Blaze can do that."

"I don't want Blaze to do it," I say, giving him a hard look.

My suspicions are my own and I don't want to put her on anyone's radar if I'm wrong. Which I'm starting to think I might be, but I've not got this far by taking chances.

"I want to know everything about her."

He takes it with a frown and opens it up. I have printed out a photograph from the surveillance video at the bar. It's a clear shot of her standing by Raven as they talk. I watched the whole thing last night to see what Cherry did when she came back out of that hallway.

They left the bar within five minutes. She was rattled, like any woman would be after how I treated her, but even I could see there was more to it.

Raven didn't question me when I took the video. I didn't want her looking back to see what I got up to in that hallway. From watching it back, it didn't look that bad. It looked like we were about to fuck if I'm being honest.

That got me fucking worked up enough to shut down the laptop, get in the shower and jerk off to thoughts of her hot little mouth. And thinking about how close I came to touching her tits.

Pushing those thoughts aside I watch Garrett looking through what little information I have. It's clear he wants to ask me about her, but he holds his tongue. Then tells me he'll have it with me within a few days, but then he is going out of town so once it's done, we're done.

I hold out a hand. We've worked together a lot of years, and we might not be tight, but we have had an understanding. He shakes it and after a few seconds he thanks me. It's about his sister, not for letting him go. He won't be paid for this job, it's his final debt to the club. We're not crass enough to discuss that, knowing this is the last bond tying us.

Once he's back inside, with one last look at the Blackhawk Ink Tattoo sign on the door, I get on my bike and pull out of the alleyway.

As promised, two days later a packet is delivered to the house. Speedway has continued to keep watch, but nothing has happened. I'm still not ready to let my guard down. I've wanted to question Jesse so many times, but he'd lose his shit with me.

There is already enough going on with him that I can't bring that doubt to his door. He at least ditched the prick he was seeing and got the fucker out of his house. He said more than once he had Cherry to thank for that.

Although he didn't call her Cherry. That's a me thing. An obsession I'm beginning to worry about. Women are complicated and as the president of a motorcycle club, complicated is not what I need.

Doesn't mean I can't take her for a ride.

"Dada, look-it," Oscar waves a white fluffy thing at my kneecaps. "Puppy."

I push the envelope behind some plant pots on the windowsill and tend to Oscar. He wants to show me a new stuffie his uncle Speedway brought him. It's a small golden retriever dog with a bright blue bow round its neck.

He's been asking for a real puppy for days now because of it. I'm going to shove my fist down Speedway's throat for putting that idea in his head.

We play for a bit and I make him some lunch, then once he's settled down for a nap, with the puppy he's calling Oscar Two, I finally get the information on Cherry.

Her real name is Taylor Crane, twenty-seven, native to Baltimore but went to college in Chicago. She lived with her father until she went to college then had her own place but moved back in with her father when he...

Shit. I lift my head up and stare through the window over the backyard. It was recent too. I vaguely recall Jesse mentioning his usual nurse had not been around for a couple of months, but I hadn't thought much of it. Why would I?

I'm well and truly interested now. Having only ever known shitty parents myself it's hard to comprehend what it must feel like, then I catch sight of Oscar's hand. It's randomly up in the air while he is sleeping, the kid is unique that is for damn sure.

If anything ever happened to him, I'd lose my goddamn mind. I only hope one day, when he's older, he feels the same. Fuck, two years ago, I never would have let emotions like this be a part of my life. What did I care about kids and their parents?

Mine and most of the people I know had assholes for parents so understanding what it must be like to lose one you actually love didn't cross my mind. From the very thorough background Garrett has provided it's clear she thought a lot of her father.

He hasn't included many photographs which isn't normal. She isn't our usual kind of target. I snap a quick picture of the two images he has got, and the one from the video surveillance, and then tuck it away for later. All of this information will be burned once I've read it.

Which doesn't take long because he's found no ties to anyone that could link her back to Chains or Storm. In fact, her only involvement with anything to do with an MC was coming to my house and then the bar and that was all purely coincidental.

She has a small circle around her that includes her job, a few friends and until his death, her father.

Raven told me the woman with her the other night is sniffing around Stryker. Good luck to her with that. He isn't much into hanging around with women. He fucks when he needs to but spares little more time for them than that. All he cares about is fighting and doing what needs to be done for the club.

Her friend is best to realize, and quickly, trying to get involved with Stryker will end in tears.

So that was why they were there that night. She only missed out on it because Stryker is all fucked up in his head over Chains. He's booked two more fights one weekend after another to get some of the tension out.

Who knows, maybe getting the little red head under him might help. Not for me to bring up. My men have no trouble finding their own pussy. I'm no fucking matchmaker.

Unless...

Shit no, I need to leave her alone. She isn't a danger to us, I can cross that off the list of people to worry about, and focus on figuring out who I need to kill.

A high-pitched scream comes from the room next to me and I jump up and run to Oscar. He's crying and reaching out his hands. I grab him up and turn around but there is no one here. It takes a second for my heart rate to slow enough to realize he was having a nightmare.

Jesse mentioned it had happened a couple of times but this is the first time it's happened with me here.

"Hey buddy, it's okay you're safe. Daddy's here, I'm here, no one can hurt you."

His little eyes are wide and looking everywhere, the remnants of the bad dream lingering. I stroke his hair and dry his eyes, reassuring over and over that I'm here and nothing is going to hurt him. His baleful little cry as he cuddles against my chest almost breaks my heart. I'm so mad he's going through this. But how the fuck do I fight a nightmare?

Maybe I need to speak to someone about it. Sheridan left me a number for his pediatrician. I will have to get Jesse to organize a visit.

I close my eyes and hug him tighter against me. I can't even take my son to the doctor. What kind of fucking life is he going to have with me as a father? I swore the second I found out about him that he wouldn't be raised around the club.

I saw things no kid should ever have to see because of how I was left there all the time. It became easy for me to fall into the way of life. I don't want that for Oscar.

No, I will protect my son against my club, no matter what happens. As fiercely as I have kept Phoenix away, I'll do that and more for my son. Starting now.

I gather up his things and take him upstairs to get his actual comfort bear, the one he can't sleep without, and he drops the puppy like a hot rock.

While he isn't looking I kick it under his changing table. If he asks for it, I'll get it out, but out of sight, out of mind.

I text Rebel while Oscar drags a big bucket of building blocks into the middle of the room, to let him know I'm not going to be around today. Oscar needs me. As much as I'm worried about the club, I have plenty of people to delegate to.

We build skyscrapers and little houses and we race little cars around them, occasionally crashing into them and knocking them down. His laughter is like a balm to my soul. This is what I needed.

A little later when he says he is hungry, I stand up and hold out my hand. As we come downstairs, taking for fucking ever because he wants to walk, Jesse comes out of the kitchen. Oscar runs to him with a squeal and Jesse scoops him up and sits him on his hip, listening to him chatter away about us playing in his room.

I didn't hear him come in, which is worrying. Jesse keeps eyeing me, maintaining a smile on his face for Oscar but something is wrong.

It's only when he sets Oscar down that I see the papers and photographs that Garrett sent, still spread out across the table. Jesse follows my gaze then turns back to me.

There is no need to ask. He's already seen them.

Chapter Nine

Taylor

I CAN'T BELIEVE I am voluntarily driving back to this place. After what happened on Friday night, I told myself the chances of running into Noah again were slim to never going to happen. Yet here I am, parking up outside the bar in Locust Point.

It looks different in daylight, even with the bikes parked out front. The church is open and people are coming and going, others making their way down the street. None of them even glance at the bar or the biker hangout next door.

Two men standing by the bikes are watching me sitting in my car, gripping the steering wheel as I muster up the courage to get out. For the last two days, I've been searching everywhere for the bracelet dad bought me. It was the last gift he got me before he died.

He was weak towards the end but before he was totally bed ridden, his sister took him to the mall to get me something special. It means the world to me. And I lost it. In the back of my mind I knew where but I searched everywhere else before I admitted defeat.

Wanting it back is more important than being worried about seeing *him* again. I did what any normal person would do, I got their number and called the bar.

A man answered. He clearly didn't work there, nor did he have any interest in the conversation. He said Raven was out, the bar opened later and maybe it was in lost and found. He then told me to come to the bar and look and hung up.

There is no way I was going back there when it's packed with bikers, so I left work after my shorter shift and drove out here. The lights are off in the bar but I'm hoping someone is inside. It's almost opening time. I can deal with Raven, she will understand and help.

Taking in a deep breath, I get out of the car and walk past the men watching me and up to the door. It's embarrassing as hell when I try to open it, but it's locked. Closing my eyes I remember why I'm here. I cannot lose that bracelet.

Someone approaches and I turn around. I didn't see all the men the other night but I'm sure I'd remember this guy. He has piercing blue eyes, that are twinkling with amusement, and curly ash blond hair. He's wearing his leather vest but has a white T-shirt beneath it that does nothing to hide his bulging biceps.

Jeez, since meeting Noah, I've been confronted with the kind of men you only see in thirst traps on social media. They're almost unreal.

"Bar won't be open for another hour." And he has a southern accent too.

"Oh." I don't want to make a return trip all the way out here. "Do you have a number for Raven? I left something here at the weekend and I'd like to get it back."

"She doesn't usually open up, one of the other staff does that. I could try to call one of them, or you can come back later?"

I glance around. It's not so bad around here I could find somewhere to grab a coffee and come back. It's not like I have plans. I'm about to speak when the roar of motorcycle engines splits the air. A whole convoy of them come riding up and I watch, mesmerized as they ride in formation, like migrating geese.

Noah is at the front. He has on one of those helmets that doesn't go over his whole head, so his face is showing. I didn't even realize people still wore those. He spots me straight away and lifts his hand. Not to wave at me, he indicates for the bikes to carry on while he turns into the parking lot of the bar.

"Oh shit," I mutter.

The man beside me laughs quietly and I glare at him.

"Looks like the Prez is gonna help," he tips an imaginary hat at me and saunters off.

He says something to Noah as he passes and I stand stock still, watching him get off the bike, his thick thighs look amazing in those jeans.

Stop it, Taylor. No bad thoughts about the bad man. After setting down his helmet and gloves, Noah walks over to me.

"What are you doing here?"

I almost say, well hello to you too, then remember where I am and who I'm talking to.

"I lost something on Friday and I think it might in the bar," I tell him.

"Bar is closed."

"Thank you for that, I hadn't noticed."

His lips lift in a half-smile. "What is it you've lost?"

"Um, a bracelet. It's important to me." He frowns. "Your friend said that Raven isn't around and the bar doesn't open for another hour. Could you maybe let me look around or, you see if its there. I called earlier and someone said it might be in lost and found?"

Now he openly smiles. "I don't know who you spoke to but I think they were either hung over or fucking with you. We don't have a lost and found."

"Oh," I look away. This is the only place where it could be, unless it's fallen off while I was out somewhere, in which case it could be lost forever. I press my lips together to hold back the emotion.

"Wait here," Noah says, taking a step back.

He probably saw me tearing up and wants to get rid of me.

"I don't have keys but I can get in the back way."

Without any further explanation he walks away. At a loss, I wring my fingers together, a nervous habit I've had since childhood. After what feels like five minutes but probably wasn't, the door behind me clicks from the inside. Noah opens it and steps back to let me in. I squeeze past him and walk into the bar. It looks different when it's empty but it's dark inside because of the blinds over the front windows.

"Any idea where you might have lost it?"

"I only sat at the table back there or when I went to the-" I cut myself off there. He knows full well where I went.

"I'll check behind the bar if you want to take a look."

We go our separate ways, and I search around where we first met Raven, the table where we sat and then I wander down the hallway to the bathroom. I half expect him to follow me again but he doesn't. I'm not sure if that is a good or bad thing. The bathroom doesn't yield any results either and my heart sinks.

This was the last place I thought it might be. I walk back into the bar and Noah looks up from his phone.

"Not there."

"I don't see anything here either, but I can check with Raven when she gets back, she might have found it and put it somewhere safe."

"Thanks, I appreciate that."

He watches me, well, more like studies me, and I can't help thinking about how he had me pressed against the wall, staring so intently at my mouth and calling me Cherry.

"How did you get home that night?" he interrupts my thoughts.

"Cab. Raven got it for us, said you had taxi drivers."

Noah smirks and shakes his head.

"What?"

"Nothing," he presses both hands on the bar and leans back slightly. "The driver might have it in his car."

"I never thought of that, can you get hold of him, if you know the company."

"Sure," he smirks again and I get the feeling I'm missing something. "Take a seat and I'll text him."

It's not in my plans to hang around but if my bracelet is in the car, I can handle it. Noah texts someone then looks back at me. He offers me a drink which I decline, because it's mid-afternoon, who drinks at this time. Bikers probably.

"There's a coffee machine, if you'd prefer."

"Actually, that would be nice, thank you."

He nods and goes to the huge machine behind the bar. As I watch his broad back, I wonder what his men would think of him now, behind a bar making coffee for a random woman. He turns around with two cups and sets one down for me, then slides over creamer and sugar. He stands back and holds his by his abdomen.

"This bracelet, it was expensive? You have it insured?"

"It wasn't expensive, no." I cradle the cup in my hands. The initial worry I felt over being around him is diminishing. He's not behaving like an ass, he isn't threatening me or staring at me like he wants to tear off my clothes. He's being normal. Kind of nice even.

"But it was a gift from someone I care about a lot and if I lose it, I'll be upset."

"Boyfriend?"

"You're really nosy you know that." He shrugs, not caring in the slightest. "My dad gave it to me."

He nods and his eyes narrow a fraction. I expect him to say something but he glances into his coffee. What is that about?

"Only thing my old man ever gave me, was a headache."

"That bad?"

"You grow up in this life, it's the way things are."

"What about your son?"

His stance changes in a split second and I remember how he was when I went to his house, how he didn't want me to see his son.

"Sorry, I shouldn't pry."

His shoulders rise and fall a few times and I get the feeling he's trying to hold himself back. Not from hurting me, I don't think he would do that. There is something else though.

"Not a lot of people know about Oscar. It's safer for him."

"Oh," I nod. Makes sense. "I guess when you're in a gang you want to protect your kids."

"A gang?" he arches a brow.

"You know, all this."

"It's not a gang, Cherry, we're a motorcycle club, we like to ride our motorcycles."

"Is that all you do?" I give him a look, brushing over the fact my heart thumped when he called me Cherry.

"Yeah," he grins. At least he doesn't look like he's going to lose his shit.

"Well, I won't say anything about your son. There isn't anyone I would tell. I don't know you or your friends or anything about you."

He nods. His phone buzzes and he checks the text and frowns. "It doesn't look like it's in the car," he says, giving me a strange look.

My heart drops for a different reason.

"Raven still might know where it is," he says, more gently than I've heard him talk. If I didn't know any better, I'd say he knows how important this is to me, even more so than I've let on while we've been looking. But that is impossible.

"It's okay, thank you for trying. And thanks for the coffee." I need to get out of here before I let him see a side of me he really doesn't need to and hop off the stool.

Noah moves around the bar and stops me before I get too far. I come to an abrupt stop so I don't crash into him, because he moved so fast.

"Raven will call soon. She knows when I need her it's important."

"This is important?" I ask, a little taken aback.

"It is to you."

"But... Why do you care?"

"I'm not heartless. Anyone can see how much it matters to you, and hell, you came all the way out here to face the gang you don't want to be around, to find it."

"I'm never going to live that down am I?"

"I'm a little insulted to be honest," he smirks again.

Both of us know it might not be a *gang*, but they're also not some guys with bikes who like to ride around. I've seen TV shows and movies about these types of places. Noah is dangerous, especially given the patch on his chest, which my eyes drop to.

He doesn't miss it either as he puts his arm out and grips the side of the bar. I'm not exactly penned in like I was the other night but he's kind of stopping me walking out.

If I wanted to. God what am I even thinking. He keeps looking at me, his blue eyes intense and heavy. The silence stretches, an unspoken pull between us. This is all wrong for me, he's dangerous but...

"Remember when I said I wanted to taste your lips?"

"Vaguely."

He reaches out with his other hand and takes hold of my waist. He doesn't tug me nearer, but it feels like we're wrapped up in some kind of bubble and only we are inside.

He keeps staring at me and I inadvertently lick my lower lip. Noah groans and then he moves, this time tugging me towards him. Before I can even think he's pressing his lips against mine.

On Friday night I would have fought him off, I probably should knee him in the balls but right now, that is the furthest thing from my mind.

He's so big, so firm as he pulls me into him and his hand moves up to the back of my head. He holds me where he wants me as my lips part and our tongues meet.

A surge of desire floods my system and I grasp his shoulder, pulling at him so he releases the bar and wraps his other arm around me. This is a kiss like I've never experienced before and I really don't want it to end. Neither does Noah as he cups my ass, pulling me against his groin. He's hard, and that almost makes me come to my senses, but he stops kissing first.

He lets out a groan as his eyes open and he stares at me.

Lord, we need to stop. Both of us need to come to our senses. This isn't right.

"They taste good," he murmurs, holding my chin to keep me close. "But I think your other lips might taste better."

It takes me a second to grasp what he's referring to, giving him enough time to lift me and set me down on the bar top. He can't be serious. His hands slide up my thighs, beneath my skirt and come to rest on my hips, pulling at the elastic of my panties.

It takes a lot but I force myself to grab his arms. He stops straight away and looks up at me. Lust is pouring out of him as he watches me.

"I don't... It's not something I usually like."

His brow lifts and something potent flares in his eyes. His lip spread into a smile. "Then let me change your mind."

He doesn't wait for a response and tugs at my panties. I have to lift for him to get them out from under my ass and I guess that's all the go ahead he needs. Me too, because if I didn't want this, I'd have stopped him.

I'm not lying, I've never enjoyed when men go down on me. Not because I don't like the idea of it, it's never felt good.

Noah takes my ankles and puts them over his shoulder. The bar is high enough that he doesn't need to get on his knees, just bend forward. I watch as his head dips and hold my breath. This isn't what I came here for at all. But I'm curious and dripping wet. Something he realizes when his tongue runs up my opening. He groans, and it makes my heart crash.

His eyes lift up to me as he takes hold of my hips and pulls me closer. I lean my arms back and grip the other edge of the bar to stop myself falling and watch as his tongue circles around my clit, lapping at me. He makes a satisfied sound then plunges his tongue into me.

My head falls back, my eyes roll and I grip the counter so hard my nails scrape across the wood. It wouldn't surprise me if they leave gouges but I don't care because he is teasing every part of my pussy, licking and thrusting, then circling my clit. He does it over and over, rotating his tongue.

A noise comes from my throat that has him laughing against me, which should embarrass me but his hot breath sends me into an even deeper frenzy. When I've done this before, it has never felt like this. He kisses my pussy the way he was kissing my mouth, like he is tasting me, like he's desperate.

A tug starts to pull in my lower stomach, my heart begins to pound and I moan again, leaning back on my elbows so my back bows.

Noah grips one thigh and pushes his face further against me, spearing his tongue deeper and flicking it, hitting a spot that I didn't even know was there. That is all it takes, I lose it and cry out as an orgasm rolls through me. I forget everything about where I am, why I came here and how upset I was. All I can feel is the aftershocks jolting through me as he continues to lap at me.

Well, he definitely convinced me that this is something I like. Or something I like *him* doing.

He pulls away but keeps hold of my hips. My legs drop off his shoulders like I've got no control over my limbs, I'm barely managing to stay upright on the bar.

He straightens up and grabs my waist helping me to sit up. I'm so flustered my cheeks are burning and I'm breathing too hard.

"Does that make you reconsider how you feel about having your cunt eaten?"

That should shock me but, coming from him, it really doesn't. It makes my stomach flutter and my pussy clench again.

"You might not taste like cherries, but your fucking delicious."

No man has ever spoken to me like this before. I'm speechless and still not entirely sure that happened. The ecstasy still flowing through me says otherwise.

His phone buzzes again, he uses a napkin to wipe his mouth and chin then grabs it from the bar beside us.

I'm still struggling to catch my breath when he takes a step back, his jaw clenching. His demeanor changes instantly. I suddenly feel a chill and close my legs.

He glances at me as if remembering I'm still here. I watch as he bends over and grabs my underwear. I expect him to throw it at me, the way he's changed, but he sets the phone down and slides it up my legs, then helps me down before setting them fully right.

It takes some of the sting of his next words away.

"You need to leave. I'll get Raven to get in touch, leave your number."

And he walks away, towards the back of the bar. I stand still, watching where he disappeared. What the hell happened? Jesus, I can't believe he walked out. He got what he wanted and then... He never got off. He only made me. I'm so confused. The roar of bikes startles me and I watch through the blinds as the bikes all pull out.

Shit, anyone walking past could have seen us. My cheeks burn even harder. A man like him is all wrong. For me, or for any woman. He doesn't want anything from me.

So I had a great orgasm, one of the best of my life, so what? I'm about to run out when the door opens and a biker steps in. I flinch in shock but he stays where he is.

"Prez said to get your number."

What? Oh... He took the time ask someone to make sure I left my number for Raven?

God don't be fooled by that. I scratch out my number on a napkin and as I pass the biker, I hand it to him, then hurry out and back to my car. I really hope Raven knows where my bracelet is because I'm still too messed up to comprehend what Noah did to me.

I might not have got what I came here for, but I definitely got something I never thought would ever happen to me.

Chapter Ten

Nero

THE BIKES COME TO a stop outside our warehouse and I get off, storming over to where Razer is waiting. He looks as pissed as I am as I take in the mangled lock on the door.

"What did they take?"

"Not a lot before the alarm triggered. Cameras caught it all, they freaked out when the internal alarm went off. They ran with two smaller crates. The beretta 92s."

My jaw clenches again as Razer pulls back the door and we all go inside, walking through the rows of shelves that hold regular bike parts and other pieces of crap that hide what is really in here.

Beast is in the back room with a couple of other brothers, looking over the inventory. I know everything that should be in here and there are two boxes missing. Each of those boxes held around five grands worth of semi-automatic handguns. All untraceable.

It's not a lot in comparison to what else is in here, but it isn't about the money.

We cannot have a real alarm going off for everyone to hear outside, but the one inside is loud enough to freak anyone out. And I'm glad it worked, together with the sensors and cameras.

"That's all they managed to grab," Beast says.

"It's two boxes too many," I growl out and walk back to the security room. "Show me," I lean over the chair where one of our newer members is, and he brings up the security footage. "Fuck."

They're covered head to toe, wearing gloves and ski masks. They suspected cameras, but they wouldn't have had a clue about our deafening security system. These two rooms are completely soundproof. I've been stood inside when that alarm went off and it felt like my ears were bleeding.

"I want to know who they are, who sent them, and where I can fucking find them."

"On it, Prez."

As much as I want to scream and yell, I keep my mouth shut and walk back through and out into the warehouse. What makes it even worse is that it's broad fucking daylight. They walked up and thought they could get inside.

No one without prior knowledge of where things are in this warehouse would have been able to go straight to that room. Rebel meets me at the main entrance. He's already instructing someone to get a new lock organized.

"This came from inside."

"Yeah," he agrees.

Neither one of us mentions his name, but Chains knew where the guns were stored.

"Whose watching him?"

"Bullet and Jameson. They said he hasn't left the garage. No calls, no emails. Just getting on with his job."

"Giving himself a fucking alibi," I grind out. I think for a moment as my men work around me to try to fix this. The more I think about it, the more it starts to bother me. "Did we have anything going on today?" I ask.

Rebel frowns. "No. Not today."

So what the fuck was this? I look back at the warehouse, at all the security around it. Rebel stands beside me, watching me.

"This was a test."

"What do you mean?"

"They were testing out our security. They grabbed what they could to make it look like they were trying to steal from us, but they wanted to see how we'd react. Check with the clubhouse and the other businesses, see if anything is up."

Rebel goes to do it. I call Jesse. He's not talking to me after he found the file on Taylor, and we had some words about it, but he won't ignore a call. My mind goes back to her lying on the bar top. I'd give anything to be back there sinking my dick into her.

Jesse answers before I can think any further about it.

"Where is Oscar?"

"Playing in the yard."

"Get him inside."

"I'm with him."

"Get him inside, Jesse. Make sure everywhere is locked up and call me when you've done it." I hang up and call Speedway. "Have you seen anything?"

"No Prez, all quiet, what's up?"

I explain about the break-in and he curses. "I'm sending someone else to sit with you."

"That means telling them about Oscar."

Fucking hell. It doesn't matter, my son's safety is more important. I tell him to make sure nothing happens and hang up when Jesse calls me back.

"What's going on Noah?"

"Nothing to worry about. I want to be sure Oscar is okay."

"That's some bullshit but I know you won't tell me the truth. We'll stay inside but he isn't happy."

"Do what you can to make him happy. Just don't fucking tell him I'll get him a puppy."

"You'd deserve it if I did." He hangs up.

Jesus Christ. I pinch the bridge of my nose. Rebel comes back and tells me nothing else has happened anywhere else. What the fuck was this about?

"How much longer before we pull Chains in?" Rebel asks.

I know why he is asking but I still think we can get more from him not knowing we suspect him. "Get Ellie to work him over."

"Might work," he says.

"She can suck the truth out of any cock," I say, making Rebel grunt out a laugh. It's not funny, and he stops laughing after a moment and heads off.

Ellie has been working at one of our strip joints since I became Prez. She's smart and beautiful and has got information out of many men for me in the past. She does it in a way that they don't even realize what they're giving up at the time.

I've fucked her a few times, the woman knows how to work a man's body and gives head like no one I've ever met before. But that is all in the past as far as I'm concerned, especially when I realized what she could do for me. It could make me an asshole for asking her to use her body like that but Ellie gets off on it. She loves deceiving men with power and stealing their secrets out from under them.

I don't know what happened to her before she started working for us but she relishes seeing men brought to their knees.

She'll be surprised Rebel is siccing her on a brother, but I trust her to keep her mouth shut. She has it good working for us, an expensive apartment, a brand new car, anything she wants to buy herself she can. Ellie is loyal, no matter how many people have tried to lure her away, she has remained part of the Blackhawk Disciples outer ring.

We get things cleared up and secured at the warehouse and head back to the clubhouse. When we pull up, the bar is open and people are inside. Shit. What the hell is Cherry going to be thinking. I was a fucking asshole who ran out on her.

Jesus, it's probably for the best that she thinks that. Still, I find myself going into the bar and heading straight for Raven, who is busy instructing a brother to change a barrel for her.

"Hey," she looks up at me. "Got your message. I had the bracelet."

"That's good."

"Found it in the hallway," she gives me a look but doesn't say anything more, she doesn't need to. "I'm meeting her friend Dana in the city to give to her. Figured you didn't want her coming back. You know, since I watched the video," she gives me an undecipherable look.

"Raven," I grind out.

"Relax, I deleted it. *Again*. But you need to be careful."

"Don't tell me what to do, Raven."

"When it comes to club business, you know I tow the line. But that girl, she isn't the kind of girl who can be around a place like this. You need to leave that alone."

"When I want your advice, I'll ask for it." And she isn't a girl. She's a fucking sexy, distracting woman.

Raven rolls her eyes, and I resist the urge to give her shit, instead heading back outside. Looking around the area my thoughts go back to this afternoon. Thank fuck only Raven saw that video, in the heat of the moment, I didn't even think of the cameras.

Wait... She's a distraction.

No. I've been through this. She has nothing to do with Chains or Storm. I trust Garrett to find out everything he could. But he did it in a hurry so he could get out of town. What if he missed something?

Why is she always showing up when something happens?

Later that night I'm still pondering that question while sitting with a few of the other brothers at Elegance, in a private booth watching a naked woman grind up and down on a pole. There is a pile of cash on the floor at her feet, which is necessary given there are no panties to tuck money into.

As I finish my drink, she wraps herself around the pole and lifts her legs, opening them so we all have a full frontal view into her pussy. I blink and look away as the men around us cheer. None of them are my officers, who she is trying to impress. All the girls vie to be the entertainment when we show up but that is crass.

I lift a hand and a waitress comes over. She has on black lingerie and an apron. "Get Ellie for me."

She nods over the loud music and walks away. Rebel has already called Ellie and told her what we need her to do. Chains is sitting at the bar with another stripper right now. I've been watching Ellie give him little looks and light touches every time she passes him.

She's the crème de la crème here and the official manager of the girls. He's eagerly lapping it up every time she shows him some attention. I shift around when she leans over me.

"Yes Prez," she purrs.

"Hey gorgeous," I smile. "Do me a favor?"

“Anything,” she winks. It’s no secret she wants us to fuck again, she practically undresses me with her eyes every time I come in here, but I’m done with that.

“This dancer,” I point at the girl who is now on all fours with her ass pointing at the table everything on show. Even some of the guys aren’t looking at her anymore, as she humps her back up and down to the music.

Ellie looks at her and scowls. Seems she is well aware of her. If the dancer has been doing this for any length of time, it should have been dealt with sooner.

“I want her gone, tonight. This isn’t what I expect of this place.” Sure it’s a strip club, but Elegance doesn’t let just any asshole walk in off the street. The cover charge to get in is a hundred dollars. Private dances cost upward of a thousand.

“Me either,” she straightens up and crosses her arms. “She’s showing off.”

“She can go show off at someone else’s club.”

“It’s done.”

“And I know you have your ways of working but are you going to handle the other situation any time soon.”

“These things take time, honey,” she gives me a grin. “But I know it’s a rush job. Have faith.”

She touches my chin and winks, and I shake my head as she walks away. No one else would get away with touching me like that. She has some balls on her.

“You’ve got some serious self-control to keep turning her down,” Rebel says.

“Been there.”

“She’s premium.”

“That says it all,” I point out, and he laughs, getting my meaning that Ellie might be discerning when it comes to who she fucks, but she does fuck. A lot.

“Fair point.”

When the song finishes, another girl comes over and speaks to the dancer at our table, she pouts but walks off the stage. The new girl is dressed in a sexy lingerie set and when she dances, I’m much happier. She’s a less sleazy stripper.

More drinks flow and everyone is happy, considering what went down today.

Rebel nudges me and lifts his chin. I glance over and see Chains following Ellie, she is holding his hand and sashaying her ass as she walks ahead of him. His eyes are firmly on her ass.

"Let's see if this works," Rebel mutters. "It's a fucking travesty the little bastard is going to enjoy himself while she's destroying him."

I agree.

As the night moves on and some of the brothers disappear with the dancers, I think about Cherry again. She's got some strange fucking chokehold on my thoughts. I've barely spoken to her, *and* I still don't fully trust her. Raven is right, she isn't the kind of woman I should be thinking about.

It's getting hard to stop. Especially after I know how fucking amazing it is to kiss her, and the way she fell apart for me after telling me no one has ever made her come from having her cunt tongue fucked. Shit that was a fucking head rush.

I'd been determined to prove to her that maybe she was waiting for the right person, which is a really fucking dangerous thought. Hopefully my running out and leaving her, left a different kind of taste in *her* mouth and she never wants to see me again.

I'm glad that she has her dad's bracelet back. She didn't want to tell me how much it meant to her and I couldn't let on that I knew.

Things with her are done.

One taste was all I got, but that is going to have to do. It's best for both of us we never see each other again.

Chapter Eleven

Taylor

Mrs. Thorne wheels her husband out of my consulting room, and I follow them down to make sure they're okay. They're in their seventies and she has been looking after her husband for the last fifteen years.

He has a lot of different illnesses as well as the diabetes and it's getting increasingly harder for her. She'll never admit it though. They've been married for nearly sixty years and never spent a night apart.

I can't imagine what that is like. It was always me and dad, he never talked about my mom unless I asked, which I stopped doing when I was around eight, because I could see it was upsetting him.

The bracelet shifts as I brush my hair back and I run my fingers over it. I've never been more relieved when Raven called to say she had it. She found it near the bathroom but didn't know who it belonged to, so put it in the safe.

I do not think about Noah, or that he came through for me with Raven. And definitely not our last interaction. I'm a piss poor liar. It's been ten days and I can't stop thinking about what he did to me.

That says a lot about what I've been missing. He *really* proved me wrong.

"They're so cute," Caitlyn is leaning against the counter watching as the Thorne's leave.

"They really are but I'm worried she is taking on too much."

"That's true love for you." She pats my arm and goes to call in her next patient.

Watching out of the window I ask Ashlyn to let my next patient know I won't be a second and run out to help. Once he's safely inside the car, I hand her a card for carer's assistance. She looks at it and thanks me.

"For as long as I can manage, I want to take care of him, it's what we promised when we got married. If I was in his position, he'd do the same thing for me. But thank you for caring Nurse Taylor. You're a very sweet girl and one day you will find your Mr. Thorne," she winks and turns away.

What if my Mr. Thorne is all wrong for me, with tattoos a motorcycle and part of a *gang?* I chuckle to myself at that thought. I sounded like such a moron. Didn't put him off though.

Long after they're gone, I stand there on the sidewalk, thinking about their long relationship. It's hard to imagine what a love like that feels like.

The sound of a motorcycle draws me out of the daydream and my heart races at the thought it might be Noah. But it's not, it's not the kind of motorcycle he rides. The man sees me watching as he slows to take a corner and looks at me until he has to turn away.

I've got more important things to do than stand out here thinking about something I can't have. Even if I already know Noah has ruined me.

I'm back to working, full clinics now so the rest of the day goes by in a blur and I'm looking forward to getting home and taking a nice long bath. One of the best things about staying in dad's house is the clawfoot tub.

When I check my last patient, it's Jesse. For a moment I panic, then remember Ashlyn always schedules a two-week follow up appointment from when I last see a patient. I just forgot to tell her it wasn't required. He's here now, so I have see him. It's insane to feel guilty but I'm still not convinced Noah isn't the guy Jesse was referring to about having a crush on. He told me it wasn't him but I'd completely forgot about it till now.

Oh God. What do I do? The door opens and Jesse comes and smiles. I can't really pretend to be busy, not when I'm only standing here. So I tell him to come through and make small talk as we enter my office.

"How've you been?" I ask once we're seated.

"Great actually. I probably didn't need to take up an appointment slot, but I wanted to make sure everything was okay with you."

"With me?" I ask in surprise. "Why would that be an issue?"

"The whole Noah thing," he says pointedly.

What? Did he tell him what we did? I can feel the color draining out of my face.

"He was an ass when you came to the house and we didn't really talk when you were leaving. I didn't want you to think I didn't care that he was being rude to you."

"Oh, honestly it's fine," I let out a breath. "I was more concerned about you. He was rude to you as well."

"Ah, that's the way we are. I've known him since I was a kid, he's like the annoying brother I never wanted."

"So he's like a brother?" I ask slowly.

"Taylor, I told you that day, he isn't the one I... you know. That is someone else. Someone Noah knows but I'm not going there, it's never gonna happen and I've made my peace."

"I feel like we should be having coffee for this talk," I laugh.

"Yeah, it's not really a medical chat. If I'm wasting your time I apologize."

"Not at all, honestly. It's nice to wind down at the end of a busy day. However, we should maybe do some medical chat. What about the situation we discussed last time, have things got better?"

"It has. Well, in that I dumped the guy I was seeing. He had moved in with me without us really discussing it, that might have been something to do with it. Without sounding like an ass myself, I'm not short of money and he was using me. Breaking up and getting him out of the apartment has eased things up."

"That's good."

"Yeah. Although I have got no one to test... on?" He laughs at the comment. "I feel better, mentally I mean. I know you said you're not an expert or a therapist. Sometimes all it takes is a logical discussion, talking things through to see what a different way of looking at things could mean. I do feel like things are going to be better. It was psychological rather than physiological."

"That's great Jesse. I'm happy for you."

He nods and smiles. "I really felt so bad about Noah though. He has his reasons for being the way he is."

Do I tell him? Jeez, not that we had a moment in the bar, just that I've seen him since. No, there is no point. I will not see him again.

"Hey, there was one other thing I wanted to say."

"Okay."

"I'm sorry about your dad. I should have mentioned it sooner, but I didn't want to pry or say anything that would upset you."

"No, that's fine. Thank you. It was hard but I'm getting there, slowly."

"I hadn't realized when I came in a couple of weeks ago. I knew he was sick. God, sorry, I'll stop talking about it.

"It's fine, don't worry. Yeah he was ill, but it took him quickly. Which is sort of a blessing for him."

"Not for you," he says sadly.

"No. It's always the living who suffer the most right."

"If there is anything I can do."

"I appreciate that but don't worry I'm good."

He stares for a moment with a strange look on his face, after a second he shakes it off and smiles again. "I'll get out of your hair. And who knows, next time I see you, my sex life might be sizzling."

We both laugh and I walk him out. That was nice, if a little odd, it seemed like there was more he wanted to say, but I'm glad he's doing better.

I'm also glad I didn't let the man he has a crush on go down on me in a bar.

"What are you looking so guilty about?" Caitlyn waggles her eyebrows. "Jesse got you hot and bothered?"

"Grow up," I push her but we're both laughing. "What time are you finished?"

"Now. I have to meet Darren in about twenty minutes, he's taking me to dinner."

"Oh nice. I've got some patient notes to finish up."

"Paperwork, bane of my existence. Have fun."

"Thank you. So much for that. Really appreciated."

Caitlyn laughs again and grabs her things.

I head back to the office and start pulling up records so I can update them electronically from my notes. Sometimes it gets like that, too busy to be on the computer, I write everything down. It's worked for me for years, even if it means staying back longer than I really need to.

Shannon pops her head in and says she will be working late too, and to say goodbye when I'm going because everyone else has left and the front doors are locked.

It's almost six when I finish up. Still early enough but the clinics finish at 4 so it's overtime but I figure it's my issue for working the way I do so won't claim it. As requested, I pop in and say goodnight to Shannon then head out.

It's a bad idea to drink coffee this late in the day but I'm beat and I have some things to do at home. There is a coffee shop a few blocks away, and it's a nice enough night, so I leave the car and start walking.

I've been going through dad's stuff because eventually I am going to decide what I'm keeping or giving away. I'm not ready to actually part with it all but I've begun boxing things up. My phone buzzes and I pull it out of my purse. It's a text from Dana to see if I'm interested in going to the Battlefield with her.

God, why is she still so hung up on this fighter biker dude? It's clear he's not interested. I type out a text and pause at a crosswalk. It's still rush hour so fairly busy.

It's why I don't notice the motorcycle riding up towards me. I'm in the middle of replying to Dana when it stops a few inches from me and the rider grabs my phone.

"Hey, what the hell," I tug on it and he fights me. He goes for my purse and I wrestle it back. "Stop, get off me."

He lunges for me and I scream as he hits me in the face. Putting up my arms to defend myself he hits me two more times and my lip splits. The final hit is so hard my head spins and I start to lose my balance. He pushes me so hard, I go down sideways, falling like a ton of bricks.

As I land on the hard pavement, I scream out again but in seconds everything goes woozy.

The man tugs my purse from arm, picks my phone up from the floor and jumps on his bike, speeding away before anyone can stop him. It happened in less than sixty seconds.

Everything blurs as tears leak from my eyes and people run over to help me. My brain is still trying to catch up with what happened while people are shouting about calling 911 and a woman ducks down asking if I'm okay.

No, I'm not okay. I'm really not.

The police and an ambulance are called, the EMTs set me on the back and treat my wounds, wrapping my wrist. The police ask me a ton of questions I barely remember. My face hurts, my wrist is throbbing, my body is going into shock.

Vaguely I hear the police talking about a spate of these kinds of assault and robberies. They ask if I can describe him but he was wearing a full helmet with a black visor I couldn't see through and gloves. I don't even know what race he was, or if it was a man or woman.

Although the force with which I was hit says it was a man.

Finally, the questions stop and I'm loaded into the ambulance. I lay back on the gurney and close my eyes, trying to get some respite from the lights. The shock will fade soon, and I will have to deal with what happened but right now, I'm fighting the pain, my whole face hurts.

I've never been hit before. I've treated people who have when I did nurse training but it's never happened to me. I wrap my arms around myself as we drive through traffic toward the hospital. It's not an emergency so there is no need for lights and sirens but the paramedic wants me to get my wrist x-rayed and check for concussion.

More tears spill from my eyes, running down my temples and into my hair. I wish with all my heart that dad was here. If ever there was a time I need him, this is it.

Chapter Twelve

Nero

Blaze sits down at the table beside me looking less grim than most of my officers have the last few days. I'm fucking exhausted but I don't have the luxury of taking a break. I've found one of our regular buyers is breaking off a deal. We've had a relationship for five years. We supply them with all their drugs but they called off the next buy. No reason, in fact the asshole hasn't been responding.

The plan is to go see him tomorrow. He doesn't know that. Or that half the club is gonna roll up at his shitty little nightclub and fucking ruin his day.

This shit is getting out of hand. Chains is proving to be more difficult to crack than any of us thought. Not even Ellie has got him to open up. I tried to call her off a couple of days ago but she is determined and has been spending most of her spare time with him.

She even told me he is thinking of her as his girl, which makes her want to vomit, but no man has ever beaten her in this game.

"What have you got?" I ask Blaze.

"Something good. Finally." That perks me up. "Ellie came through."

"Seriously?"

"Chains has a burner phone. While she was fucking him senseless, she slipped it to me and I cloned it, got it back to her before his dick was barely out of her."

"Not a visual I needed."

"You and me both. Ellie can be very descriptive."

"What's on the phone?"

"It's been quiet for a couple of days, but some texts came through last night. They were about Cannon." The club owner who pulled out of our deal. "I've not been able to trace the number he's talking to and they erase their texts straight after they go through but I got screen shots."

He hands over the phone and I read through the messages, my jaw clenching. I should be happy, this is the fucking break we needed as far as Chains is concerned.

Blaze sits silently and watches me as I think. Rebel has been telling me for a few days that sitting back and waiting isn't working. He's still worried about the trial run at the warehouse and expecting something to go down. We've stepped up security there, and at some of our other businesses to be safe.

With this new information, we have something we can confront him with. "Get Fury in here."

Blaze nods and I hand him the phone. He leaves me alone and I rub at the headache growing in my temples. There is no evidence he's communicating with Storm, but it makes sense. Watching him has shown us he's gathering men around him. Assholes and ex-cons, people you can't trust further than you can throw them, but he somehow has their trust.

All the evidence is mounting up against him. This text exchange means we can get Chains locked up and find out what the fuck is going on. Blaze calls to say Fury is in the city but he's heading back. I head downstairs instead of moping upstairs. The big screen TV is on and Zephyr, one of the old timers is dozing on the couch.

He is well past being able to be a part of anything that happens in the club but he is such a fixture here, I've not had the heart to tell him it's time to step back. He doesn't have anywhere else to go, always sitting here watching TV.

A news report is on as I grab a bottle of water from the fridge, I glance up at it as a reporter is talking about another motorcycle attack. That piques my interest and I walk closer, not that I need to the size of the fucking screen. Motorcycle attacks, what the fuck does that even mean?

A roll of photographs show people who've been hit, and at the scenes as they talk about smash and grab attackers, pouncing on unsuspecting pedestrians, stealing phones mostly.

Fucking assholes, that pisses me off. Gives us motorcycle riders a bad name. I almost laugh at my own joke when they talk about their latest victim. A photo comes up. It's not a close up, and I'm not even sure she knows it's been taken.

My heart pounds and I hurry closer grabbing the remote. Just before the story goes off I pause it. "What the fuck?" I grind out, making Zephyr snort awake.

He looks up at me and sees the rage pouring off me. It's nothing new, but this is a different kind of rage. This has consumed me as I look at Taylor sitting in the back of an ambulance with blood running down her face and her eye swelling. This happened two days ago.

I toss the remote and pull out my keys. "Tell Fury I'll text him later," I call out to Zephyr.

The club should come first, there is a lot of shit about to go down but I can't stop myself from going to her. I barely know her and this is insane, but I'm so fucking angry. I have her address from the file Garrett gave me and don't care she might ask how I know where she lives. All I care about is getting to her and finding out what the fuck happened.

Before I pull away I text Blaze asking him to find out everything about this.

When I find the little asshole who did this, he's going to fucking pay.

Her dad's house is about twenty minutes north in Hampden and I make good time getting there because I'm breaking all kinds of laws. It's difficult to disguise my arrival given it's a quiet residential street.

Taylor's car is parked out front, there is no driveway and the front lawn is a little overgrown, separated from her neighbor with a chain-link fence. Before I get off the bike my phone rings.

"I've got footage of the incident," Blaze says. "It's bad, fucker attacks this woman like he enjoys it."

"Send it to me. I want to watch it."

"I'll condense the file."

"Whatever with the tech stuff."

He agrees and while I watch the house, an email comes. I open the video and watch, there are a few camera angles as it plays. First Taylor is walking up the street, she is in her nurses uniform and she looks happy, carefree. She takes out her phone and smiles broader as she is texting.

Then the motorcycle comes into view. Blaze has put it together so I can watch him coming, see how he stops and takes note of her. Then it switches to another angle, the back of Taylor as she approaches the end of the sidewalk, waiting to cross.

The bike races forward and stops right in front of her. According to the news these crimes are about opportunity. He snatches her phone and reaches for her purse, shocking her. He should leave but Taylor puts up a fight. Part of me is proud, but another is telling her to let the shit go, it's material things, her safety matters.

"Fuck," I growl as he gets off the bike and grapples with her. Then he hits her in the face. Her head is knocked sideways. Rage like I've never experienced fills my body as I watch him hit her again and again. The people around stand and fucking watch as Taylor falls to the ground.

I can watch that part later, I keep my eyes on him as he grabs her things and runs back to the bike. Blaze followed his escape for a while with CCTV footage. Then it goes back to her. Passersby are helping her now. And she's fucking crying.

I'm going to tear his head from his fucking neck. It takes a moment for me to calm down, as I pocket the phone. Taylor doesn't need to see me like this.

I get off the bike, walk up the path and jog up the steps onto the porch.

Now that I'm standing here, I don't know what the fuck I'm going to say to her about why I'm here. I can't stop re-running the image of him hitting her beautiful face. Without a second thought that it's a woman, or that he has fucked this up and should run. No, he got off his bike and...

A curtain behind a small window on the front door moves and Taylor peers out. Her eyes widen when she sees me. The glass is opaque but I can still make out most of her features.

"Open the door," I tell her.

"What you are doing here?" she asks.

"Do you really want to have this conversation through a door?"

"You should leave, Noah."

Hearing her call me that kick starts a heavy beat in my chest. Only Jesse calls me by that name these days. Even Phoenix and my mother call me Nero.

"Open up Cherry, I'm not going anywhere."

Her head lowers, and she doesn't move for a moment.

"Cherry, you either open up or I'm going to let myself in."

"What is that supposed to mean?"

I reach up above the door and feel around, then look at the planters on the window and go toward them. If I know these kinds of houses and the type of man her dad was, there is a spare key here.

"Okay," she calls out.

The sound of locks undoing and a chain sliding make me stop searching. We'll be having words about that too. It's not the sixties anymore, it's not fucking safe to leave a way into her house when she lives alone.

The door opens a crack, she still isn't letting me in.

"Cherry," I lean an arm on the doorframe and try to see her but she is hiding her face.

"Noah, please leave."

"You know why I'm here."

"I'm fine."

"You're really gonna leave me standing out here? I'm not going away. And your neighbors won't be too happy when I bang on the door, or rev the bike to get your atten-"

"Fine," she cuts me off. "Don't do that."

"All you gotta do is let me in."

She steps back and opens the door and I walk inside before she can change her mind. I close the door and she wraps an arm around her middle, looking toward the back of the house. The front door opens up right into the living room with a staircase on the right.

It looks like a guy lived here with an old but comfortable looking dark couch, and matching chair. There is a large TV facing the couch, a coffee table and rugs. But I'm not interested in the fucking décor.

Taylor is still not looking at me. There is a heavy bandage on her wrist and hand, only her thumb and tips of her fingers sticking out and I see red.

Tamping down the rage, I step closer, she still refuses to look at me, so I reach out carefully and touch her chin. "Look at me."

"It looks worse than it is."

"Cherry, look at me."

She must hear something in my voice, and it's not anger or an order. It was quiet, almost gentle. Nothing like I'm used to hearing from myself.

Slowly she turns her head and I keep my fingers on her chin, holding it up as I study every bruise, every cut and mark on her beautiful skin.

It takes a hell of a lot not to curse but I don't want to scare her. She is still hugging herself. The embarrassment is clear, and she's trembling slightly, but she doesn't need to feel that way. Not around me.

"What have the police done?"

She shrugs. "The surveillance footage wasn't clear and I couldn't describe what they looked like."

So nothing then. They were right. The footage is clear enough for me to see the tears running down her broken face, but not any way to identify the rider. Blaze won't stop until he finds him.

"It's been happening a lot apparently. I'm not the first. I appreciate you coming but... wait how did you know where I live?"

"Not important."

"It kind of is," she frowns, a bit of the Taylor I'd seen the first time we met slips out.

"We'll worry about that later, I want to know everything about what happened."

"You think you can do more than the cops?"

"I know I can."

"Noah... I don't want you to do anything crazy."

"What makes you think I'll do something crazy. Cos I'm in a gang?"

She rolls her eyes, then winces.

"Fuck," I sigh and take a step closer. Taylor watches as I slowly stroke my finger around the bruise under her eye, careful not to touch it. The colors of the bruise are at that horrible purple green stage, and the cut on her lip is healing but still looks sore.

She closes her eyes, and a tear falls from between her lashes. Her chest hitches as she struggles not to let her emotions get the better of her.

I'm going to murder him for even daring to touch her.

Around us, there are reminders of her father everywhere, pictures, an old sweater on the chair, and it dawns on me that she is here alone. I might have a shitty dad, but Taylor didn't. All I can think about is how relieved Oscar was after his nightmare when I held him and soothed him and without thinking, I wrap my arms around her and pull her against my chest.

Taylor resists for a moment, her body tensing but I don't give her a chance to pull away. It's selfish and I might be an asshole for doing it because she barely knows me, but something tells me she needs this. After a while, she leans into me and I wrap my arms tighter around her back.

Her little sniffs and the dampness seeping through my shirt tells me she is crying. I can't fucking stand this but I refuse to let her go. I'll stand here and hold her as long as she needs it. There is more to this outpour, this is about her dad too.

I'm really fucking confused about how I've ended up here and what it means.

When she moves back and wipes at her eyes, I guide her over to the couch. She sits down, keeping her eyes off me. I glance through the dining room to a kitchen and walk through, searching through the cabinets till I find cups.

There is tea on the counter beside a kettle, not something you see often. I fill it with water and set a tea bag in the mug. Something I learned from one of the older-timers old lady's a while ago. Taylor doesn't move except to pull a blanket around her shoulders and she stares at me when I come back with two steaming cups.

I'm not a tea drinker, but what the hell. She needs to know I'm here for now.

"You have anyone who can look after you?" I ask, handing her one of the cups and sitting down beside her.

"I hardly need looking after," she laughs.

"The wounds might be superficial, Cherry but the trauma isn't."

"I don't want to talk about it."

"Have you turned people away?" I lift a brow.

"I can take care of myself. You're the only one who hasn't taken no for an answer."

"That's my modus operandi."

Her lip tilts slightly, but it falls as fast as it came. She looks bone tired, especially after letting out all that emotion.

"Have you been sleeping?" She shrugs. "Nightmares?"

"What are you doing, Noah?"

"Being alone after something like that isn't good for you."

"You're hardly the person I'd expect to help."

I ignore that. "When did you last sleep, Cherry?"

"Last night," she says but her eyes dip away, a sure sign she's lying.

There is a lamp on a side table at the end of the couch which I flick on then get up and turn off the main lights. Taylor watches as I come back and adjust some of the cushions, then get back on the couch closer to her than before. She doesn't know what to say when I put my arm up around behind her.

"Just don't ask any fucking questions."

Her brow lifts.

"You're not sleeping because you're alone."

"You don't need to stay," she starts to protest.

"I mean this in the nicest possible way, but shut up, lie back and go to sleep."

"I'm not tired," she argues.

"Then I'll give up, but not until you try."

"Who even are you right now?"

"Let's say neither one of us are who we normally are right now and leave it at that."

Taylor stares at me and I do my best not to get mad at the bruises. I'm not sure I hide it but Taylor doesn't comment, instead she leans back against my arm and I shift to cup her shoulder, then pull the blanket up over her chest.

At first she sits still and I keep tilting my head to see what she's doing. It takes about ten minutes for her eyes to start to droop. I've been around people who've taken a beating too many times not to know what they need. Eventually, she falls asleep and I stay still for a good half hour until I'm sure she is in a deep sleep.

The whole time I'm re-playing that video in my head, thinking about how I intend to kill that fucker.

It takes some finesse but I manage to get my phone out and send messages to Rebel, Blaze and Jesse. Giving my men orders and asking Jesse to take care of Oscar for me.

He's still pissed at me, but where Oscar is concerned, he'll do what needs to be done. Rebel replies saying he will make the arrangements for going to Cannon's club tomorrow and let me know what time.

I'm not planning on leaving her alone. Whatever this pull she has on me I'll question some other time. I'm pissed she's told her friends she is okay when clearly she isn't, and they haven't pushed to stay with her.

It's quiet here and after a while, my eyes start to drift too. It feels like it's been an age since I've sat, not having to go anywhere, not having to deal with a multitude of problems, or people expecting something of me.

My phone buzzes, startling me out of a doze, and I grab it quick so it doesn't wake her. Taylor shifts, turns toward me and cuddles against my chest, the crown of her head under my chin. The blanket slips a little and I have a perfect view straight down her top. Fuck me. I pull the blanket back up and look at my phone.

Blaze: I've tracked the bike to an address in Mid Town and Mount Vernon. I've sent Daze and Vicious to check it out

Nero: Make sure they know I want to deal with him myself

Blaze: Okay. I'll find more info on the owner and who he hangs out with

I put the phone down and look through the front window. Then shift carefully to make sure I don't wake Taylor as I get up. Once I'm sure she's still out, I make my way around her house, checking everything out, including the security measures. The outdated security system and flimsy locks on her window don't fill me with confidence.

What is clearly her dad's room is full of boxes, some full, some waiting to be made. A few doors along I come to Taylor's room. It's feminine but not overly so, and has been decorated since she was a kid, it's not a childhood bedroom.

Before things get too creepy, I pull back the covers then go downstairs. Taylor is still asleep. I'm not sure this will work without waking her but the couch isn't that comfortable. With great care, I slip my arms underneath her and lift her up.

She wakes, disorientated as I cradle her in my arms.

"Noah?"

"Relax, I'm taking you to bed."

"You haven't even bought me dinner yet," she mumbles, making me laugh. "You can put me down," she says sleepily.

"No thanks."

She moans and leans into me again. Fucking hell she is going to be the death of me.

"I'll be okay now I've had some sleep."

"It wasn't enough," I walk around the top of the stairs and into her bedroom, carefully setting her down in the bed. "You need more."

"It's okay," she starts to get up. "I'll be alright," she looks around the room then back at me, as if she isn't sure how she got here. "Um, you can go."

I stand back and look at her as she sits up, like she is about to get out of bed. Before she can get to her feet, I walk over and stand right beside her so she can't get up. Her head tips so she can look at me.

"You're worried about nightmares."

She shakes her head and turns away.

"Cherry," I take her chin and pull her face back. "Do you want me to stay so you can sleep?"

She shakes her head, but it's because I'm practically a stranger. Even though I have somewhere I need to be, I don't like the idea of her suffering alone. While she watches I take off my cut and kick my boots into the corner.

"What are you doing?"

"Shush, Cherry."

Her mouth opens and closes but she doesn't know what to say and watches me get into the bed on the other side.

"This is... Am I dreaming?"

"You will be soon, lay down and come here," I lift my arm. I don't even recognize myself right now but that is okay. I'll worry about that tomorrow.

After a few moments of hesitation, Taylor moves into the center of the bed but out of reach of me putting my arm around her. Whatever works for her. She lies on her side and watches me. I turn away and stare at the ceiling.

"You're not like I thought you would be."

I don't answer and we lay in silence. I shut off my mind and close my eyes, thinking she will do the same but before I can check on her, I fall asleep.

Chapter Thirteen

Taylor

Last night feels like a dream. Which I expect to be confirmed when I wake up and the sun is shining in through the curtains. There is no way Noah showed up at my door, looking like he wanted to tear the world apart when he saw my face, and then cuddled on the couch with me.

The bed shifts behind me and a heavy arm comes down over my waist, tugging me back against a warm, hard chest. And, oh... a hard something else. It's biology, that's all. Nothing else.

Shit, Noah is still here. I mean of course he is. "His dick is digging into my ass." I whisper.

"Yeah, it is," his voice grumbles behind me.

I mouth 'shit' and close my eyes, trying not to move and rub against it. He stretches and lets out a manly moan that has my thighs clenching and my mind going back to the bar. I should turn around, thank him and say he can go now but I don't move.

For the first time since I was attacked, I've managed to sleep through the night, because of him. He was a different person last night, he surprised me. I need to think of something to say but my mind is blank, racing and confused.

"What are we going to do about that?"

My eyes snap open as Noah shifts his hips and his dick slides against the crack of my ass. I'm only wearing the thin pajama pants I had on when Noah knocked on the door. Part of me wants to turn around and tell him to get out, I didn't let him stay so he could do this.

Then another overpowers that voice. He came here last night to check on me, and realized, like no one else, I can't sleep. Every time I close my eyes, I see a man with no face, hitting me over and over.

"Hey," a tattooed hand brushes my hair back from my face and pulls it behind my shoulder. "Breathe," he whispers, propping himself on one elbow so he can lean over me.

"Sorry."

"Don't apologize, Cherry. You don't have to say sorry to me."

His hand is stroking through my hair and my eyes sweep closed. How can he make me feel so safe when I know he is dangerous? And I'm terrified of a man on a motorcycle who hurt me, when that is what Noah rides.

He takes my chin and turns me to face him. I want to cringe away knowing how horrible my face looks but my eyes lock on his and it's like I'm trapped, and can't look away. His jaw is tight as his eyes roam over the damage but where his hands are on me, they're gentle.

He's such a dichotomy. He could be really bad for me. But as he rolls me onto my back and runs his hand through my hair, I don't try to stop him.

"I found boxes in the other room," he says.

I close my eyes and try not to cry again. I did enough of that on his chest last night.

"My dad, he passed away recently."

Noah doesn't say anything straight away. "The bracelet, that's why you came looking."

"It was the last gift he bought me before..." I trail off. I take a deep breath, not sure why I want to tell him. He listens as I talk about growing up with my dad, how close we were, how we lost him to cancer. How *I* lost him.

Noah doesn't ask questions, just listens. He doesn't tell me he's sorry like every other person who has ever heard about him. He strokes my hair and watches me with the kind of intensity I'm not used to. I feel drained again after all the talking and spilling my guts to this total stranger.

He's not quite a stranger. Not anymore. Why isn't he saying anything?

Instead of talking, he lowers his head and kisses the side of my mouth, away from the cut. It surprises me and I stare into his eyes before he lowers his head again, trailing kisses down my chin and jaw. I tilt my head so he can suck on my neck. I let out a sigh as his kisses get harder, his tongue tasting my skin.

"Fuck, Cherry," he groans as his hand trails over my t-shirt and cups my breast. "Let me make it better, let me make you feel good. You're not alone." He toys with my nipple so it hardens.

I moan as he slips his hand under my shirt and his fingers move over my bare skin. He shifts so his hard on is pressing against my thigh now.

All I can think about is touching him and before I can second guess myself, I move my hand between our bodies and do it. He hisses as I stroke him through his jeans. He lets me for a few strokes, then shifts up on his knees and tugs at my t-shirt. I sit up to get it off and he throws it behind us.

Noah takes off his own shirt, then lowers over me, skin to skin. He trails his lips over my collarbone and down to my breast, sucking my nipple between his teeth.

"Oh God," I moan.

"No, it's Noah."

I'd tell him not to be facetious but I'm too lost in the sensation of the tug on my nipple as he sucks it again. Neither of us speaks as he slides lower and slides down my pajamas and panties all together, his eyes moving over my body as his hands follow. My head tips back as he settles between my legs, lifting one of my thighs over his shoulder.

"Still think having your pussy licked and coming is impossible?" he asks, lightly stroking a finger over my clit. With his other hand he opens me and my cheeks heat.

"Answer me, Cherry," he demands.

"No," I breathe out.

"Do you want me to make you come again?"

Yes. I don't speak it aloud. His expression says he's waiting. "Yes," I tell him.

My mouth drops open and I arch up as he spears his tongue inside me. His hands glide up my stomach and he grabs both breasts as his shoulders push up against me, forcing my thighs up and wider apart. He slides his body with the movements of his tongue, undulating against me so my hips rise and fall.

The sensation of his tongue pressing in and out and the way he is tugging my nipples starts to set me off. This is embarrassing how fast it's happening after what I said last time, but that thought leaves my head as my whole body tenses.

Noah doesn't let me move even as I try to fight against it and pull him in at the same time with my thighs.

"Oh God," I cry out as pleasure rolls through me in waves and I let out a long, low keening sound.

My brain is still trying to compute what the hell just happened when Noah goes up on his knees looking down at me with hooded eyes. "I said, it's Noah," he growls.

I'm too caught in the aftershocks of a mind blowing orgasm but at the same time, I don't miss how beautiful he is as I take in the man looming over me. There is a roaring lion tattooed on his arm and he has ridges and muscles like I've never seen in real life. A thin layer of hair covers his pectorals, and I reach up to run a hand over them, making him hiss as I touch his nipples.

He shakes his head and for a moment I think he's having second thoughts, then he pulls on the waistband of his jeans, popping the buttons. His dick springs free and I can't help but stare.

He's smirking when I look back up at him.

"Is that..." A giant metal ball through the end of his dick? It's not actually that big, but I wasn't expecting it.

"Don't worry," he strokes a finger into my pussy again making me jump. "It won't hurt. Not in a bad way, anyway."

He moves to the side and pulls off his jeans and underwear then pauses with a frown. Oh, right. I lean over and open my bedside drawer. There is a box of condoms in there. For a minute I wonder how long they've been there, but when I look up at Noah, his face is thunderous.

"What is that look for?"

"Nothing," he grabs a condom and tears it open with his teeth. "Spread your fucking legs, Cherry. I want to see that dripping cunt."

My throat tightens as I try to swallow. His words are so crude, but the whole package is turning me on. I want to tell him to screw the condom and get in me already but that is a very stupid idea.

Noah gets it on in record time and lowers himself over me, his hands beside my head on the pillow. He hovers there for a moment, looking down at me.

I get lost in his eyes, they're so blue and intense and I curse the split on my lip because I want to feel his mouth on mine. He does one better though and dips his hips, entering me in one hard thrust, enough that I shove up the bed.

"Oh fuck," I cry out as he retreats then pushes in hard again, making me jolt.

"Hold on, Cherry," he guides my hand to the headboard. "Don't let go."

I grip the metal bars with one hand, the other is useless in the bandage but I keep it above my head, even though I desperately want to touch his hot skin.

His voice is commanding and damn, do I want to obey. He starts to thrust into me, his eyes locked on mine the whole time. I grip the bars tighter, pushing against his hips. He grabs on to them and holds me down, moving on to his knees so he can get more power behind his thrusts.

"You're fucking gorgeous, Cherry. So tight, so fucking wet me for. You like being fucked hard, don't you, baby? Fuck I've wanted inside this pussy since the second I saw you."

"Yes," I hear myself moaning. "Yes. Harder."

He growls and lifts my hips so I'm practically off the bed, only my shoulders are on the mattress.

"You walked into my house and thought you could tell me what to do didn't you? I wanted to show you that no one talks to me like that. To put you on your knees and shove my cock down your throat until you choked on it."

I start to lose my breath.

"You drove me fucking wild. I fucked my hand thinking of you that night."

The fantasy is a lot different to the reality but I'm picturing it as his dick pushes in and out of me. The piercing is hitting a spot deep inside of me and I start moaning, unable to stop myself.

"That's it, squeeze my cock, Cherry, oh yeah, fuck. I want to fill you with my cum, Cherry."

I can no longer speak and almost lose it when he pulls my legs up over his shoulders and leans down. He starts to kiss me and my lip tingles and then splits. Noah doesn't care, he keeps devouring me with his mouth as he pushes into me, my legs are up around his ears now and it's hitting me so deep I can barely breathe.

The friction and tightness are like nothing I've felt before. He is so fucking good at this. No one has moved me around like this, or spoken to me the way he does.

He rises slightly and there is blood smeared on his chin. He groans and starts to pump into me harder and faster and I go over again, screaming out as the pleasure drives me to madness.

"Fuck, fuck," he groans and pushes deep inside, holding still as his cock pulses.

For a brain melting moment, I wish he wasn't wearing a condom so he could fill me up the way he said he wanted to.

I'm pretty sure the sound of my heart beating is echoing around the room, it is definitely the only sound filling my ears, to the point I barely hear him talking.

"Shit," he is panting hard and his head dips, his lips pressing to the side of my breast, his tongue licking over my nipple. "You're fucking perfect," he murmurs against my skin.

He finally lifts his head and looks at me, his brow creasing as his hand comes up and wipes at my lower lip. He looks remorseful for a second then leans in and kisses me again, softer this time, but somehow more possessive than any other kiss I've experienced with him.

When he pulls back, and sits up, I lower my arms. He takes the forearm above the bandage and his eyes harden as he carefully sets it down onto my stomach.

His nostrils flare. God, is he going to get up and leave like he did last time. I'm not sure my heart can take that. Not that my heart is involved here. It would be hard to take if he did, that's all.

Noah takes off the condom, tying it off and putting it on the bed beside us. I'll worry about that later. He wipes his mouth and stares at the blood for a moment then looks back down at me.

"Are you okay?"

I wasn't expecting him to ask me that. I nod. He leans forward and lifts my head, gently pulling my hair out from where it was trapped. His touch is gentle, which is insane after how hard he fucked me.

"Yes," I whisper. "I'm good."

He smirks, like he's proud of himself. He should be. That was pretty much the best sex I've ever had. But I won't tell him that.

He sits back again and lowers my legs so they're around his hips instead of up in the air. Running both hands along my calves and the backs of my thighs he stares at me in that intense way he has, where he means every word he is about to say.

No man has ever stared into me so deeply. It's like he owns me.

"I'm going to find him."

"What?" I snap out of lust induced haze.

"The bastard who did this to you. I'll find him."

"How? The police said there isn't enough evidence."

"I'm better than the police, Cherry," he grabs the headboard and leans over me. My hand automatically goes to his chest. "He's going to pay for touching you."

I want to ask what he means, but deep inside, I already know.

And... I'm not mad about it.

I think.

Chapter Fourteen

Nero

Taylor is in the shower and I'm still sitting on the bed, dressed and staring into the open drawer by her bed, at the box of condoms.

How is it possible I'm jealous of a fucking box? Because I want to know every single asshole she has used them with. Tear the fucking hands of each man who has touched her before me.

I want to take the box and throw it in a fucking fire. Which is insane because if she hadn't had them, we wouldn't have fucked.

I've learned my lesson when it comes to being safe. As much as I would never regret Oscar, I don't want to be one of those men who has kids with different women. Like my father. Although I'm screwed in that regard, if I ever want more, because it definitely won't be with Sheridan.

Fuck what am I even thinking about. I grab my cut and boots and head downstairs. I don't need to be in the room when she comes back out of the shower because I'm likely to bend her over the bed and fuck her again. I don't have time for that.

I'm not going to bother lying to myself, it will happen again. I don't know for how long, or when I'm going to have to move on, but I want her.

It worries me that she knows about Oscar. Women have got attached to me and tried to screw me over. If she tried to hurt me through him I'd have to handle it.

That thought makes me feel like fucking shit. My phone vibrates in my pocket and I grab it, checking the stairs for Taylor.

"Yeah?"

"It's more than this one guy," Blaze says. "And we might have a problem.

"Meaning."

"They're a gang. Not in the traditional sense, they're fucking college kids, from rich neighborhoods."

"They're doing this for fun?" I grit out, my mind racing. "What's the bigger problem?"

"His dad is a district court judge."

"Shit..."

"It's up to you. Stryker has never had a problem with high-profile targets."

"He put his fucking hands on her."

Blaze is silent, he would never ask, but I did slip up. No one knows about Taylor. I don't have to explain the things I do or ask my men to do, they follow orders no matter what. But this is different. It is a problem. They need to know why I'm doing it if we take a district judges son off the map. And I intend to. He is not only getting a beat down.

The fucker is a dead man walking.

"You know who the rest of them are?"

"Yeah."

"Okay, well, they need to be fucking stopped but we can't let them know it's us. Not if we're dealing with this prick."

"Understood. I'll go talk to Stryker."

"I want to be there, for him."

It goes without saying so he doesn't respond to that. "Anything else, Prez."

"No."

Blaze hangs up. The whole time I was talking I had one eye on the stairs. Taylor might think she knows something about who I am, but what she does see barely scratches the surface. I'm not a good man and she deserves better.

I should walk out the door, take care of the fucker who hurt her and never see her again. But I've always been a selfish bastard. She's a good fuck.

Damn, it's not even that. There is something about her that draws me in, that makes me want... *something*. I want to protect her.

"Everything okay?" Taylor asks, she is standing midway down the stairs, holding the railing with her good hand.

Seeing the bruises on her face again hardens my resolve. I don't care how we do it, that kid isn't going to see another fucking sunrise.

"I have to go. I have a lot to do," I take a deep breath, and she comes all the way down the stairs but doesn't approach me, she watches me watching her.

"Thank you," she says, breaking the prolonged, somewhat awkward silence growing between us. "For coming around, and staying. I feel a lot better for the full night's sleep."

"Is that all you feel better for?" I arch a brow and her cheeks flush. "Come here."

For a moment it doesn't seem like she is going to move, then she takes the few steps across the room till she is standing in front of me. I stroke the backs of my fingers over the bruising, careful not to touch the delicate skin but enough for her to know I haven't forgotten what I said.

She needs to know who I am. If she can't handle that, then this is going nowhere. I feel bad for re-splitting her lip, but tasting her blood did something to me too. Fucking hell. I take out my phone and open the contacts then hand it to her.

"What?" she asks.

"Put your number in there and I'll text you so you have mine. If you need anything, you call. It might not be me who comes, but I will send someone."

"Noah, that's... you don't need to do that."

"Don't argue with me, Cherry," I push the phone at her.

For a second, it looks like she is going to argue and I'd welcome it right now, cos I like it when she's feisty. She blows out a sigh and taps her number into the phone. It says a lot about what the attack has done to her. I fucking hate leaving her alone, but I have no choice.

I walk to the door and she comes to see me out. "What if someone else can't give me what I need?"

My head whips around to her. The thought of one of my men being near her like that.

"You know, if I need someone to make me the perfect cup of tea."

"Cute," I narrow my eyes at her, and she tries to hide her smile. "You need someone to fuck you, I'm the only one coming round." Her breath hitches at that. "You're having nightmares," I add, getting more serious. "Same thing."

Her head ducks but I grab her chin and lift her face up. I don't need to say more, she understands. I need to leave before I do something stupid. And I need to get my mind into a whole different gear.

Outside I go straight to the planters on the windowsill and dig around until I find the spare key. Taylor watches me put it in my pocket. I'm about to turn away when she starts to laugh.

"What?"

"Dad had the door changed a few years ago. I didn't even remember that key was there."

"That isn't funny."

"It's a little funny," she tries to stop herself laughing. "And I'm not sure we're at the key swapping stage anyway," she gives me a sassy look then goes inside and closes the door.

The locks snap into place which goes someway to appease me.

And fuck me, I'm smiling as I walk down the path to my bike.

Going against what I really want to do, which is keep Taylor out of things, I will tell Blaze about her. I want a security system set up at her place, and Rebel has to know because he's my VP. If anything happens to me, it's his job to pick things up. Keeping secrets from your VP is bad news.

At the clubhouse I'm not happy when Rebel tells me we need to deal with the Cannon problem before the idiot wannabe bikers terrorizing the city.

"How did we not hear about this?" I ask him walking to the back room where the weapons are all locked away.

"Only a few have reported it to the cops. They've been getting more violent which is how it's made the news."

"Fucking assholes," I snarl as I unlock a safe and grab two handguns, handing one to Rebel. Every gun in here is untraceable.

"Are you sure this is the route you want to take with them?"

"I don't give a fuck who his daddy is, he beat her, he scared her. She's having fucking nightmares."

Rebel frowns. "Shit Nero, I didn't even know there was a woman on the radar. You're this fucking crazy about it, when the hell did this happen?"

"I'm not talking about it."

"If it affects the club."

"Fuck," I rub a hand over my hair. "I don't even know if it's serious, I don't think it can be. She's just... Fuck."

"You've said that," Rebel grins.

"She's Jesse's fucking nurse," I mutter.

"Shit," Rebel says, watching me as I pace. "Well, that's fucking messy."

"Yeah, like I said, I'm fucked," I shove the gun into the holster under my cut. "Let's leave it at that."

He starts to laugh as he takes the gun I offer and grabs another, loading up his holsters and locking the cabinet.

We meet the others out front. Rebel has already filled them in on what is happening tonight. As everyone gets on their bikes, a whistle makes me pause. I wait for Blaze. He's not coming tonight, I've got him working on other shit.

"Chains got a text," he says grimly.

"And?"

"They know we're coming."

This is some kind of ambush? My fists clench as I look toward. "Where is he?"

"In the bar," Blaze says, his own face full of rage.

I call Rebel over. Blaze tells him what he told me.

"We're calling it off, but we're not letting him know that. We ride out, Blaze watch the fucker, see what he does. Text me if he tells them we're on our way. Rebel get a couple of guys to drive out there. No bikes. They don't engage, we need to see what we're dealing with. Where's Stryker?"

"He went up to the farm to get it ready for your other thing."

"Tell him we have someone else coming up there instead. I'll come back once he thinks we've gone to the club."

"Prez."

"I said, *I'll* come back," I snap at Rebel.

He nods and glances at the bar. "Raven?" He's anxious about his sister. He doesn't need to be, Raven would smash a bottle over Chains' head if she knew what he's done.

"It'll alert him if she leaves. I'm not going to give him a chance to do anything. Blaze you, Gunner and Ronin be in there and be ready. It happens fast and quiet, no alerting the regular customers. Keep people away from the back hallway."

Everyone agrees to the plan and we get back on our bikes. I look in through the front window of the bar to see Chains sitting on his traitorous ass, laughing at something one of the other brothers is saying, throwing back a shot as he does.

"Motherfucker," I grunt.

As the engines all start and we move into formation, the little bitch looks over his shoulder and the laugh turns into a sly as fuck smile. The others move in close behind me before I get to see if he takes out the phone. But Blaze is there watching.

So many fucking assholes I need to deal with.

The real problem is Storm. How I'm going to deal with that shit is what I need to start planning for. Getting a look at the crew he has around him will help. First, we have a traitor to break.

Everyone is confused when we pull over but no one questions it. We rode a mile out to be sure. Rebel refuses to allow me to head back alone and pulls Nashville over to fill him in. As the sergeant-at-arms, part of his job is to protect the Prez, act as a bodyguard. I've never asked that of him but he can handle it if he needs to.

We ride back toward the clubhouse but pull into the back lot of the church so as not to alert anyone we're here.

"This shit is messed up," Nashville says as we walk around the back of the bar. "I know he's working with the fucker, but setting us up like this? What is he gonna get from it?"

"That's what we need to find out. And fast."

"You think Storm is planning to take us out?"

"I think he's always been planning something, only now he's found an idiot to sacrifice so he can get what he wants."

"What's the plan?" Nashville asks when we go in through the back of the clubhouse and I fill him in as we walk into the corridor that connects to the bar.

I text Blaze that we're in place, he replies, 'two minutes'. We stand quietly in the dark corridor and wait. The door opens, light spills in but we're around the corner out of sight.

"What do you mean something went wrong?" Ronin asks.

"I don't know," Blaze replies sounding panicked.

This is part of the plan to make him believe Storm has got the drop on us.

"Fuck what's happened? Are we gonna have to go out there? We need to kick their asses if they're going against the club."

Sonofabitch. That he even has the fucking balls to say that shit. Blaze rounds the corner first and steps behind me, Chains is next, and he stalls when he sees me. He looks confused, his head turning this way and that, not sure what to do.

It's clear when he realizes he's fucked cos he goes to pull a weapon, but Ronin and Gunner are behind him and grab his arms. Nashville takes his gun and I move to stand in front of him.

"What is this, what's going on? Prez?"

"Before the end of the night," I snarl. "You're gonna wish you'd never heard the name Storm."

A moment of fear flashes before his eyes before I pull back and hit him right in the center of his face, knocking him out cold.

"Van's out back," Blaze says, not even the slightest bit bothered by the sight of Chains hanging limp between our two brothers, blood pouring out of his mouth.

They drag him through into the clubhouse and throw him into the back of the van. Ronin rolls him onto his stomach, grabs his hands and zip-ties them behind his back. He does the same to his feet, then pulls a black bag down over his face.

He gets out and slams the door as Nashville and I get into the passenger seats next to Blaze.

Fury and Rebel catch up to us when we're halfway to the farm, staying behind us all the way.

This was not the problem I planned on dealing with tonight, which means that asshole gets one more day of his normal, pathetic fucking life.

He doesn't know the devil is coming for him. And if I don't get what I want out of Chains, he's going to feel my wrath even harder.

Chapter Fifteen

Taylor

I've lost track of how many patients have asked about my cuts and bruises, and bandaged wrist. I've made up a stupid excuse about falling off my bike. No one needs to know I don't actually own a bicycle. It's better than saying I fell down the stairs, that will only get their brains working in the wrong direction.

I also don't want to share that I was attacked by a psycho on a motorcycle. It's bad enough that Noah figured it out after seeing the news report. I contacted the news station after he left to tell them to remove the footage of me or I'll sue them. Drastic maybe, but I don't want my image out there for anyone to see.

All last night and this morning at the clinic I've been thinking about Noah. It's alarming that the threat he made against the person who hurt me isn't what is re-playing over and over. The man knows how to take care of a woman. In more ways than one.

My focus can't stay on how he made me feel when we woke up yesterday. Not when I'm coming to understand how dangerous he is.

I've looked up the Blackhawk Disciples. There isn't a lot of information about them on the internet, but from some deep and probably obsessive investigating, I learned a few things about them. From suspected crimes to their support and involvement in the local community.

The church across from the bar speak particularly highly of them. How can everyone think they're so violent and dangerous yet a church praises them?

His road name, which I've also been educated on about MCs, is Nero. I looked that up too, and can confirm he is in fact strong and vigorous like the meaning of the name. There I go again thinking about yesterday.

I can't put the two sides of him together. Nero the leader of an MC who no doubt does very questionable things and Noah, the man who came to make sure I was okay. The man who held me so I could sleep without being plagued by nightmares. The father to a gorgeous little boy, and friend to Jesse who he genuinely cares about, even if he was an asshole to him that first day.

When he said he didn't want anyone to know about his son, I thought it was weird. I get it now, after seeing the truth of who he is.

He sent me a text last night that said 'save this, Cherry' which made my stomach swoop and my cheeks heat. I mean, I don't wear anything that smells like cherries, but he seems to have fixated on that and I can't forget what he came up with it in reference too.

It also helps he listened to me about dad but didn't try to make me feel better with words I've heard a million times before. No one has comforted me quite the way he did.

Oh God. I need to focus on work. At least Shannon said I could still come in. I've mastered covering most of the bruising with make-up.

It soon becomes too busy to spend any more time thinking about Noah.

Caitlyn walks me out to my car at the end of my shift. I try to tell her she doesn't need to, but she pats my arm and says if she was in my shoes, she'd hope for the same. I love that she isn't being overly sympathetic. Regardless of what Noah thinks, my friends have been there for me.

Dana wanted to stay at the house but I told her no. She spent enough time here after dad. I don't want to inconvenience her again.

Once I'm locked in the car, I take out my sunglasses because it's a gorgeous day. A text makes me pause in starting the car.

Noah: I have sent a couple of guys to your place, don't panic when you see them

Taylor: Sent them for what?

Noah: They're going to upgrade your security

Taylor: Noah, you can't do that

Noah: Can and am

I try to call but he cuts it off, and another text comes straight away.

Noah: I'm on the road, Cherry. Just let them add some new locks on the doors and windows I'll hold off having a whole security system fitted

Taylor: You're not doing that.

Taylor: Why are you doing this?

Noah: I want you to feel safe again. They'll have a box of cherries so you know you can trust them GTG

That almost makes me laugh, in reality it isn't funny. I slouch back in the seat, not sure how I feel about this. It's not like anything happened at the house. I don't dare say that, he might decide to have his men follow me around.

I gnaw on my lower lip thinking about that. Would he do that? Does he care that much? We barely know each other, except in the biblical sense. That introduction has gone way beyond strangers running into one another a couple of times.

When I get home, as he said, there are two motorcycles parked out front with men standing beside them. They're wearing leather vests like Noah's and as I get out of my car, they nod like they know who I am. One I recognize from the bar that day opens a bag and holds out a box of cherries with a grin.

Jesus Christ.

I take it and introduce myself asking their names. I relax a tiny bit more. They follow me inside, one of them carrying a toolbox. The one called Nashville smiles politely at me.

"We're putting some extra locks on the windows, changing the deadbolts front and back and putting a new lock on the door."

"I don't need a new lock."

"Prez asked for it."

"Let me guess, he asked for a copy of the key."

Nashville doesn't answer that. The other guy seems quite stern and hasn't said more than his name. Nashville on the other hand is more open, and he smiles to reassure me.

"I'll take all copies of the keys," I tell him. "You can tell him I decide who can enter my property."

That gets another smile, this one much wider, then he follows the other guy. I stay back as they work their way through the house, remaining on edge until they finish up in the kitchen. Ronin leaves and Nashville brings over the keys. Both sets. I make him swear that is all he has.

"How about I let you tell him about that," he winks. "Preferably before we get back to the clubhouse and he asks for them."

When they leave, I lock the door, admiring the shiny new locks. The annoying thing about all this, dad would approve. He'd want me to feel safe here. After checking the rest of the house, not that I expected they've done anything additional, or gone through my things, I head back down and send Noah a text letting him know they've been.

My phone rings, surprising me.

"Everything good?"

I contemplate not telling him about the spare keys but don't want his men to get into trouble. "If you want a key to my house, it's going to take a lot more than changing the locks."

"That so." I can hear the smile in his voice. "Well maybe I'll swing by soon to collect."

"Maybe I'll let you in."

He laughs. "I gotta go."

"Wait about the... what you said the other day."

"Don't worry about that, Cherry. By the way, a picture of you eating one of those would be nice."

He's trying to put me off asking, and it's kinda working. "Not a chance."

"I'll see you soon, Cherry."

He hangs up before I can say anything else. I blow out a long, heavy sigh my eyes landing on the box of cherries. No, I shake off the idea. If he wants to watch me eating a cherry, it is going to have to be in person.

The following day I'm off rotation at the clinic and Dana comes round to keep me company. Dana has been with me through so much shit the last few months, she's been a godsend.

She helps me upstairs going through dad's things and gives me hugs when I need them. She keeps eyeing the bruises and asks what the police are doing. I haven't heard anything from them so I doubt much.

"Bastards need a taste of their own medicine," Dana mutters. "You know they've been doing this a while. Other people are coming forward. It's like an epidemic or something."

"Do you think there is more than one of them?"

"It has to be, they're happening all over the city. Oh, honey are you okay?" she shuffles closer when my face drops at the thought.

"I'm fine," I wave her off. She's not convinced quickly but I smile and hand over some old shoes of dad's for the goodwill box.

My mind is racing, but not because of what Dana said. If there is a whole group of them, what is Noah going to do? I mean, he said he's going to make the guy who attacked me pay, but how will he know who he is if there are more of them? I really don't want him getting into trouble over me.

When we're finished Dana tells me we need to get it over in one go, rip the band aid off, so we load up her car and take everything to a local Salvation Army. They're grateful for the donations and Dana chats with them as I watch them put the boxes behind their counter.

It's another step in the cycle of grief. Seeing his things go on to help others less fortunate. Dad would like that. He was always giving to charity and looking out for people.

It's hard, seeing his things go, knowing I'm never going to see them again. But like Dana says, they're only things. I've kept the important items, pictures, his watch and signed baseball collection. I'll never let those go, but this is really hard.

"You okay, honey?" Dana comes over, she hands me a tissue which I use to wipe my eyes and nose, nodding but not having the words to respond. "Let's go home, listen to some nineties love songs and bake cupcakes."

"That sounds like a horrendous afternoon."

"*Sooo* horrendous," she over-exaggerates the word and links my arm tugging me back to her car.

The house smells of vanilla and chocolate and we made good use of the cherries topping off the frosting with them.

"Only problem is, who is going eat them?"

"Not my fat ass. We can take them to work tomorrow. Do you have a container?" She goes looking and pauses, staring at the back door. "New locks?"

"Oh, um. Yeah."

"What's that uncertainty for?" she side-eyes me in that way Dana does when she knows I'm hiding something from her.

I don't want to lie and use my attack as an excuse, that wouldn't sit right. The only reason I went to that biker bar at their club was because Dana is interested in one of the men and he never showed.

How will she take it that the actual *President* changed my locks? Among other things.

Dana is my best friend and I kind of need to talk to someone about it.

"Okay so, something happened."

"Something like what?"

"Remember I lost dad's bracelet?"

"Yeah," her anxiety at my initial statement changes to curiosity.

"When I couldn't find it, I figured the only other place it could be was Raven's bar."

"Oh... Ohhh." Her mouth hangs open

"And um, I might have ran into Noah... I mean Nero."

"Nero, the President?" she asks incredulously. "Wait a second," she holds up a hand. "Did you call him Noah?"

"Well, that's kinda how I know him."

"Girl you better sit your ass down and tell me what the hell is going on and how you've managed to get yourself on a first name basis with the President of a motorcycle club."

She punctuates that by pointing at me, then the chair. It's not like I don't get where she is coming from. Who am I kidding, this sounds really bad.

"Well, it all started when a patient needed a ride."

Chapter Sixteen

Nero

"He talking yet?"

Rebel looks tired, like the rest of us as he joins me at the table. We've spent the last two nights working over Chains but not got anything worth shit out of his sorry ass. I'd left them last night to keep trying so I could go home and see Oscar.

"No. Stryker isn't holding back either."

That's hard to hear. On the one hand, we need to go beyond the usual roughing up to get the answers we need, but Chains is Stryker's blood relative. It's good to know my Reaper's allegiance to the club is greater than blood loyalty, but I'm not totally heartless.

"Juice managed to tail one of the men working with Storm. Blaze is working on getting more information about him. It's a fucking shame Ghost has ghosted us," he chuckles at the joke, then shakes his head. "Would he help?"

"I'm not pulling him back in, I gave him my word. We can do this without him."

"Just saying..."

"Not happening. Unless it gets really dire, but I'd rather leave that alone."

There is so fucking much going on right now I wanted to take a minute to get my shit together. There is always someone coming in and interrupting. I've spent a lot of fucking time, too much if I'm honest, thinking about Taylor. It's been two days since I went around to her house.

I'm trying to put her out of my mind, she doesn't need me and my shit invading her life. It's really fucking hard to do that.

"Where are we with the college dickhead?" I ask.

"It's time to pull Stryker off Chains, let the fucker stew a while. I'm sure he can be ready to go."

"We need to make it look like something separate to what happens with the rest of them."

"What are you thinking?"

"Something out of the box. It involves the cops."

Rebel blows out a breath and leans back. "In what way?"

"Give the names of all of them involved, except him. I want them to think he turned on them."

"Smart."

"I've been known to come up with a good idea or two," I smirk. "Let them think he's fucked them over. Give Maguire his name so he can slip it to a few of them when they're being questioned. Sew doubt. Their families will probably get them bailed out. If they think he turned on them, they might do something stupid."

"You want to let them take him out?"

"No, but if they try to fuck him up, then it won't look so suspicious when he disappears."

"Got it. I'm due a catch up with Detective Maguire, anyway."

"Thinking about Cannon too," I stroke my chin, the stubble is starting to get soft. "Maybe they're overdue a raid."

Rebel laughs. It's not usually how we work but if it stops Storm in his tracks stealing one of our customers, then it's worth it.

"Ask Fury to switch things up with Chains, try to find out about the deals they're making rather than what their bigger plan is. Who they're talking to."

"Make it look like Storm's crew gave something away and fucked Cannon over. Have other people know he can't be trusted," Rebel adds.

I nod. This is why we work so well together, he can follow my train of thought without me having to explain it.

"Anything to fuck Storm up is good by me. Not gonna lose any sleep over it."

It goes without saying nothing leaves this room. We have a few cops on our payroll but Maguire has been working with Blackhawk for nearly ten years.

Crash, my predecessor, cultivated that relationship and I kept it up, paying him well. He's done a lot of shit for us over the years. If he's ever found out, he'll be sent away for life and probably killed while in there. That's why I want to keep him safe.

An anonymous tip to the narcotics division is all we have to do for Cannon's club to get raided.

It's more delicate with the biker gang. It may not be as fast as I want it to be, but it will be worth it. Anything I can do not to tip my hand to Taylor helps. I wish I hadn't said the fucker would pay. She's a smart woman, she will have put it together what I am by now. And not just another gang.

Which is why I'm surprised later when I text her that she not only replies, but invites me over. I should say no. If I'm going anywhere, it's home again to be with my son, but the pull I feel towards her is making me doubt my decision.

Maybe one last time, to tell her it's not happening, we're not right for each other. Yeah, cos I'm big on talking about shit like that. Fuck it. I gather up my shit and let Beast know I'm not contactable for the next few hours but I'll check in.

I've got all the brother's checking in regularly. Given Storm's grand plan got fucked up, we have got to be vigilant. I'm already breaking my travel in pairs rule. Shit, what the fuck am I doing going to her house. If anyone is following me, I'll lead them right to her.

I pause and tap out a message to Jesse. It's a lot to ask given how much time he's been spending with Oscar. He agrees to take him overnight. I'm sure he knows why but isn't asking questions, club business rarely comes to my home.

I let Speedway know what's happening, and he's going with them, although Jesse's place is like Fort Knox, I still feel better knowing someone is watching over them.

Taylor takes a while to respond to my message for her to come to my place and my inner voice is telling me it's best if she disagrees. I'm parking the bike when she messages to say she's on her way.

I grab a quick shower and tidy up Oscar's stuff. Although Taylor is aware of my son, I don't need to leave reminders of him on show.

The file Garrett gave me on her was destroyed, I learned from that mistake when Jesse saw it. He didn't buy my excuse that I was doing the background on her after she saw Oscar, he told me to stay the hell away from her. If only I could. Hell, I don't fucking understand it either.

When she arrives, I open the door wearing a pair of sweatpants and if the way she looks at me is anything to go by, it's very much appreciated. She looks hot as fuck in a little black dress. It's nothing fancy, a casual wrap dress with flat shoes, but her legs are on display, and there is a hint of cleavage that has my mouth watering.

The bruises on her face have faded a lot but she could have also covered the worst of it up with make-up. Her split lip has healed up better.

It would be wrong to grab her and fuck her against the wall, even if that is what I'm picturing. I welcome her in and she follows me to the living room.

"I was surprised you asked me over," she says, setting her purse on the floor by the couch.

"I'm surprised you agreed."

"Why?"

"You going to say you've not asked questions about me, or looked me up."

Her cheeks flush a little.

"What did you find out?"

She shrugs. "Not a lot that went into great detail, but I can read between the lines."

"And you still came?"

Her breath comes out on a slow exhale, and she looks as unsure as I feel. "Looks like."

My smirk grows into a grin. Now that is out the way, can I bend her over the couch? "Do you want a drink?" I say instead.

"What do you have?"

"Depends on what you feel like."

"Vodka?"

"The heavy stuff, huh?"

"Why not?"

Well, because she came in her car, which means she is expecting to stay. Alright then. I get us the drinks and bring in a mixer in case she wants it but she downs a shot, making me arch a brow.

"Can you tell me anything about it, or what I'm getting myself involved in."

"You don't believe in beating about the bush do you, Cherry," I turn sideways so I'm facing her.

"Life's too short," she replies. "I'm not saying I expect anything," she quickly adds. "I'm nervous about this."

"Do I scare you?" I ask bluntly.

"No," she replies. "Maybe I should be scared, but I'm not. Not of you."

"You should be scared. I won't lie, Cherry. I'm not going to tell you anything about the club. That is the way it is in my world. And I'm the President, so I'm pulled into everything, night and day. The club will always come first."

Taylor chews on her lip and looks down into her empty glass. This is the right thing to do. Scaring her wasn't in my plan tonight, I was fully on board with fucking her all night. It tells me everything I need to know about my feelings about Taylor.

Any other woman and I'd happily have used her body to get what I want. She's different and should be pushed away.

I'm broken out of my thoughts by Taylor leaning forward to set her glass down on the coffee table. My heart sinks for some stupid reason. This is for the best. She takes my glass, and I lift my eyes back to her as she stands up and steps in front of me. I shift back so I'm facing her as she nudges my knee so she can step between my legs.

It's on the tip of my tongue to ask what she is doing but I stay tightlipped. Her hands move to the tie at her waist and she undoes the bow, letting her wrap dress fall open.

Fucking hell, all I can see is a tiny scrap of transparent fabric between her thighs, I can see the neat patch of hair and my mouth starts to water.

She slips the dress from her shoulders and it pools at her feet. It's taking great fucking restraint not to touch her, but this is her moment.

My chin tilts upwards so I can watch her face as she unclips the bra. It's front fastening which I've never seen before and shit do I like it, because it opens up like a fucking gift, her tits spilling out of it. She stretches her arms back to let the straps fall down to the floor behind her, jutting her amazing tits towards my face with the motion.

The only thing I move are my eyes as they lower down the perfection of her body. Her hands slip into the side of the elastic at her waist and she pushes it down, stepping out of them one foot at a time. It reminds me of the strippers at the club but I brush that thought away fast.

Taylor is nothing like those women. She isn't doing this to impress me, or to gain clout for having stripped for or fucked the President. She's never once called me Nero, like those women who don't even know my real name.

I'm not a good man. My head is telling me to make her dress and go, instead I reach out and put a hand on her hip bone. She shivers from the touch as she watches me glide it down over her outer thigh, feeling the silky soft warmth of her skin.

She lets out a small gasp when I trail it back up the inside and ghost over her pussy, not dipping inside, just a featherlight touch across her clit, and up her stomach. When I reach the underside of her tit, she moans. It's time to test her.

I sit back and pull the sweats over my ass, tossing them aside. Taylor's eyes fall on my rock hard cock and I wrap a hand around it to get some fucking relief from how painfully hard it is. When I look back up at her, she reads the question in my eyes, and responds how I want. By dropping to her knees.

For a second, it crosses my mind to get her a pillow, but I'm not that nice. She leans forward and brushes my hand away, replacing it with her much smaller one, but her grip is strong and I hiss as she strokes me. It's fucking torture watching her as she works her hand up and down.

I'm about to shove her head over my cock when she looks up at me.

"Can I taste you?" she asks, looking everything like the sweet and innocent girl I know she isn't.

It makes my balls tighten, those words in that seductive voice.

"Get those cherry lips wrapped around my cock before I lose my fucking mind."

She smiles then bends forward and takes the head in between her lips, sucking and licking it like a lollipop. It's nice and all but not what I want right now. Placing a hand on the back of her head I push her down. She obliges me without complaint swallowing down half my cock. I keep pushing and she gags but doesn't stop, her hand wrapping around the base.

Now she knows what I want, I loosen my grip, and she bobs up and down, taking me in further, moving faster. My head tips back on the couch and I stare up at the ceiling as she works my cock. Fuck, she is good at this. Her hand slips between my legs and cups my balls, making me thrust up and further into her throat.

She chokes and pulls back a little. I'm tempted to tell her not to fucking stop, but she goes back to licking and squeezing me. Just watching her is making me fucking hot. I reach down her back and stroke her ass, pulling her forward so I can tease my fingers between her crack.

Taylor moans and spreads her legs, making it easier for me to dip inside her wet pussy.

"Fuck," I ground out as she swallows me down deep again. I can barely take this anymore. I'd love to fill her throat with my cum but I'd much prefer to be inside that sweet cunt when I do.

I take her shoulders and push her back. She almost stumbles when I get up and grab her under the arms and lift her, then without warning throw her over my shoulder, making her squeal. I grab a handful of her ass and march out of the room, up the stairs and into my bedroom.

There is no chance for her to look around before I toss her on the bed, grab her hips and spin her so she faces down, her legs hanging over the edge.

"Stay there. Don't move."

She looks at me over her shoulder, her eyes hooded and lips parted, watching me grab a condom and pull it on. I walk back to her like a predator and her throat works as she swallows.

"You ready for me to fuck you, Cherry?"

"Yes," she says, her voice strong.

I lift her hips and put her knees on the bed then bend mine to the right level and shove inside of her, the tightness of her welcoming the intrusion, making her cry out. Oh yeah, this is so much better than her mouth, even though that was amazing. I fuck into her hard, and she straightens her arms to make her stance more rigid, so I hit as far as I can as she pushes back.

My focus goes solely on her ass, and watching my cock disappearing and reappearing, the condom glistening. I'd give fucking anything to tear it off and feel the real her but my brain instantly dismisses the idea. She's begging and moaning the harder I thrust and I lose all self-control, rutting in and out like an animal.

Taylor claws the comforter and starts making a loud keening sound, then cries out as she clamps down on me. I fuck her harder, needing to feel that climax tearing through her, until my cock can't take anymore and I pump everything I have into the condom, into her.

"Fuck," I lean my head down on her spine and try to catch my breath. She stays pressed upwards, taking the weight of my body as I bend over her, wrapping an arm underneath her waist. We can't stay like this forever, though the thought of pulling out of her irritates me.

The condom takes over any decision I want to make about that. It's practically full. I step back and remove it, tying it off and going to the bathroom.

When I come back out Taylor is sitting on the end of the bed. She looks up at me, hesitant.

"Don't look at me like that, Cherry," I tell her. "Ten minutes and I'll be spreading those legs again, but first," I get on my knees and push my face between her thighs. She flinches back but I grip her hips and pull her into me as I suck her clit into my mouth.

"Oh God... Er Noah," she corrects.

"Damn fucking right," I growl, then press my tongue inside her. "Now wrap those legs around my neck and show me how much you want to get this pretty pink pussy tongue fucked."

Chapter Seventeen

Taylor

The temptation to ask about his son has been consuming me. Well, after he went down on me until I felt like my mind splintered, then lifted me up, walked to the wall, pressing me against it and fucking me like that.

Noah did not stop until he had me screaming his name. He's like a machine, I've never experienced anything like it. The last thing I thought would happen is us lying in bed together after all the sex. He strikes me as the type who showers and dresses and sees a woman out and not with a thanks for the good time as the door closes behind you.

I'd been expecting that and am kind of still waiting for the other shoe to drop. Letting my stupid heart read more into that would be insane. It's not like we're cuddling or anything.

Dana had plenty to say about what I've been doing. She said with no irony whatsoever given she was panting after a club member, that I needed to stay away. Her logic made sense. Stryker isn't President. But what difference does it make, really? They're both a part of it.

Dana tried to fill my head with horror stories but all I keep thinking about is him holding his little boy, getting him what he needed and helping to settle him. Like a true, caring father.

It reminds me of my dad, but I can't let memories of him into this room with us. That feels all kind of wrong given what he did with my very willing body.

Noah is sitting up drinking a glass of water, the sheet draped over his lap. I can see the outline of his dick the fabric is so thin.

Hard to believe that has been inside me, it's big and the piercing... He wasn't wrong when he said it would hurt in a good way. I'm feeling particularly tender right now. Even if I wanted to, I'm not sure I could do it again.

"What are you thinking about over there?"

My head snaps up from the pillow. I'm lying on my side, staring at his dick. He's smiling like he knows exactly what I'm thinking when I meet his gaze.

"What is the difference between the President and guys who are part of the MC?"

His brow lifts. "Didn't I tell you earlier I wouldn't talk about the club?"

"The way I see it," I shuffle up, pulling the sheet with me so it covers my breasts. "I'm asking about the hierarchy of a *hypothetical* motorcycle club."

"When I'm the president of one?" he cocks his head.

"Yeah," I bite my lip to hide the smile. He's amused too, he can't hide that.

"Well, the word President says it all, don't you think. It's the CEO of the company, in charge of everything, oversees employees, makes decisions and keeps everyone in line."

"That's an unexpected analogy."

"Best you're gonna get."

"So everyone else is like your staff?"

"There are higher ups," he muses, finishing his water and setting it down. "Board members you might say," he shifts onto his side and puts his elbow on the pillow, so his head is level with my chest.

"And they all have roles."

"You've looked it up, don't pretend you haven't. It's easy enough to find how shit works on the internet."

"Okay, fine. I did that. Where does Jesse come into it?" I ask cautiously.

Noah sighs and rubs his forehead. I'm about to say it doesn't matter when he answers me. "Best friends since we were kids. He's too good to be in the club and he didn't want to be, anyway."

"What makes him different?"

"He isn't soft exactly," he looks at my expression and frowns. "It's got nothing to do with his sexuality. I don't discriminate like that, not in my club. People are free to be what they want to be, so long as they're loyal."

"That's weirdly admirable."

"I'm an admirable kind of guy," he smirks. "Jesse isn't cut out for the life. And he has his medical issues."

"So his sexuality doesn't hold him back, but his disability does?"

"This life is hard sometimes. Jesse wouldn't be able to cope if someone got hurt because of him. We don't exactly have an HR department, Cherry."

"You're the one who used the office analogy."

He snorts a laugh.

"What?"

"That is so far from what it's like."

I nod. We're quiet for a moment, each lost in thought.

"At the root of it, we're a family. Our bond is sometimes thicker than blood. A lot of members have no one, or come from bad backgrounds. They get what they need being a part of the club."

"That's sweet."

He sits up again, his expression incredulous. "Did you call my MC sweet?"

"I called you sweet, actually."

He bursts out laughing and nudges my leg. "I hope you always think that, Cherry."

His laughter fades and we get lost staring at one another for a moment. He blinks out of it first and lowers his eyes. I'm still covered by the sheet. He slowly starts to peel it back. I really am tender down there but pulsing heat coils low in my belly from the way he watches as my body is revealed.

He presses a hand to my inner thigh, and it pushes my legs wider, looking at me down there. He blinks and looks up.

"Are you sore?"

I'm surprised he asked. "A little."

He pushes my legs back together and pulls my hips so I lay down flat on the bed, then he straddles my waist and grabs my breasts, massaging them and teasing my nipples. They harden within two seconds of him touching me.

"Love your tits," he mutters, dipping forward to suck on my nipple. "I'm going to fuck them."

"What?" My surprise isn't hidden.

He moves back and drags his cock up my midriff, letting it rest on my chest. Then he presses my breasts together, trapping it between them. "Like this."

He pauses and leans over, grabbing a bottle from the bedside drawer. I watch as he pours the lube over himself and it dribbles onto my chest.

My heart is pounding as he tosses the bottle, then massages me, before trapping his cock again. I clutch the sheets as he starts to thrust, slowly at first, his eyes locked on mine.

I've never done this before but watching the intensity of his beautiful face as he starts to thrust a little harder has me melting into another dripping wet puddle. I shift my hips trying to get a little relief for myself.

Noah is so lost in what he's doing he doesn't notice that I'm close to telling him to fuck me properly.

"Hold them," he tells me, grabbing my arms.

I push them together and he grabs the headboard and starts fucking himself harder in the channel I've created. When he groans and tips his head back, warmth gushes over my chest and throat, spilling down my neck.

I don't even care that he came all over me, especially when he pulls back and starts to rub it in, holding my neck as he leans in to kiss me. He doesn't stop, laying himself flat over me, his tongue rolling with mine.

It's not hurried or charged with lust like his other kisses have been. It's consuming and makes me feel lightheaded. I grip his hips, partly to anchor myself to something real, because this kiss feels different to anything else we've done. More intimate than him being inside me.

Eventually he slows and dots open-mouthed kisses on my cheekbone and jaw. I'm convinced he is about to lap up his own cum when he pulls back. He takes my good hand and lifts me up so we're standing by the bed.

He gets a feral look in his eyes as he stares at my collarbones. He almost says something but clamps his lips together and leads me to the bathroom. He turns on the shower and encourages me inside. I'm somewhat disappointed when he doesn't join me, but it's probably for the best.

Something in the way he looked at me makes me need space. I'm certain he feels the same.

When I get out of the shower, the bedroom is empty but my clothes are laid out. I stare at them, knowing what that means. I'm stupid for being disappointed. He's made it clear what he's like.

This felt like more than sex, more than it was last time.

Maybe that's why he's doing this.

A noise at the door startles me. He's wearing jeans and a T-shirt, watching me as I try to pull back the thoughts of him not wanting this to continue.

"I got a call," he says.

"Oh, right." I turn my back to dry myself off and pick up my underwear.

The warmth of his body makes me straighten up. He's right behind me and he snakes an arm around my waist, pulling me back to his chest.

"Believe me, I'd rather stay here but like I told you before, the club always comes first."

I twist my neck so I can look at his face. I see it in his gaze, he's telling me any life with him would be this way. What surprises me the most is that I'm not upset about it. Not now he has pulled me against him.

There could come a point when he leaves me in his bed to go. Stupid, stop it.

He brushes my damp hair back then kisses my forehead. "Get dressed, Cherry. I'm not leaving till your safe in your car."

"It's just outside."

"Don't argue with me."

"Yes Mr. President."

He frowns at that and I feel like I massively messed up. In my head it was supposed to be like a kink thing. When it comes to his club, I guess there is no joking around. He taps my ass and tells me to get a move on, then heads out to let me get dressed.

Why am I such an idiot? My cheeks flush with embarrassment and I throw on my clothes, hang the towel back in the bathroom and head to the stairs. I pass by a bedroom and glance inside to see a crib and some toys. It makes me soften again.

He might think he's the big bad scary president, but he has a baby he loves, and a best friend he looks out for. He's gone above and beyond to make sure I feel safe after that asshole hurt me.

He's waiting by the door holding his helmet and keys and my purse, which he passes to me.

"I'm sorry about that flippant comment, it was stupid."

"It was fine, don't worry about it," he rubs a hand through his short hair. "I try to keep it separate from this house. Things are different here. Does that make sense?"

"Yeah," I nod. He doesn't need to explain it is about his son. "I won't do it again."

He smirks and I flush again at the assumption I made that I'll ever be here again. Get me out of here now.

I duck past him and open the front door. He follows me, laughing and I give him a haughty look over my shoulder.

He walks me to the car, and I expect him to grab me and assert some kind of authority but he stays back, looking down the street. There is nothing else for me to do but get in the car. Before I fully close the door, I tell him goodnight.

"I'll text," he says.

My heart flips over, but I contain my shit and nod instead, closing the door. Noah doesn't move until I'm driving away, I keep watching in the rearview mirror as he gets smaller, standing there, watching me drive away, and I wonder what he is thinking. If it's the same thing as me.

It's going to be really hard to walk away from him.

Chapter Eighteen

Nero

THE SOUND AND SMELL of this place really does make me want to gag. As I climb off the bike I glance to the left where the pigs are. Some of them are inside their barn but a few are out snorting around, digging up mud and hay with their snouts. There is nothing nice about these pigs, they've survived on human flesh and bone for a long time now.

I don't know how Stryker stands it. He doesn't live on the farm, he has two trusted people who manage the place and take care of the pigs, even breeding them to make sure there is a never-ending supply. They're never around when Stryker is busy with his late night work or anyone from the club shows up.

I'd give anything to still be with Taylor, my plan had been to keep her in my bed all night, something I haven't wanted to do in years. I can count on one hand the number of times a woman has slept in my bed.

It was different when I stayed at her dad's place, she was vulnerable. I wanted to let her know she was safe. Fucking her for the first time the next morning was a bonus.

Once again, I have to compartmentalize my thoughts and not bring myself here with her on my mind. Chains is finally talking.

I wince when I walk into the large barn that is way at the back of the land, away from the small farmhouse and the pigsties. It doesn't last long because this fucker is a traitor. Still, seeing someone hanging from the ceiling with meat hooks through his shoulders isn't a sight anyone should get used to.

Apart from Stryker. He has no issue doing this kind of thing. The place smells of piss and blood. Razer and Nashville are standing off to the side talking as I walk in. They both look up and move toward me. For now, it looks as if Chains is unconscious.

The closer I get, the easier it is to see the destruction of his face. I'm not even sure his nose is where it's supposed to be. It is sickening, but what this prick did is deserving of it.

"What else did he say?"

Nashville stops beside me, hands on his hips as he looks at Chains with as much distaste as me.

"Had we gone to that meeting two nights ago, it would have been more than an ambush. They had M16 assault rifles and were going to mow us down as we drove up."

My jaw clenches. They didn't plan on showing their faces, like the fucking cowards they are. I'd turn around and punch the fucker myself if I thought it would hurt. He's out cold and I'm not sure any hit I could give will rival the world of pain he is already in.

Out of the corner of my eye I spot Stryker sitting on a hay bale in a dark corner. If I were anyone else, I might have jumped seeing him there, so still and quiet. I'm used to finding him like this, sitting and watching, his face a blank mask.

As Nashville fills me in on the plan Storm had to take us out and how Chains was feeding him everything we were doing, I watch Stryker watching me.

Some people say he has dead eyes, but that isn't what I see when I look at my Reaper. I see a man who needs to do the awful things he does because he's afraid of himself, and what he thinks he might do to those around him, the people he cares about.

I don't know what happened to him in the past, or the weight he's carrying, all I know is, doing what he does for the club keeps his monsters at bay. Now he isn't sure what to do. Those two things are colliding here, his cousin is now the enemy.

Shit. I shouldn't have let it get this far. Stryker's jaw tightens, and he wrings his hands together, the knuckles all busted up. I lift my chin and after a beat, he gets up and walks toward the door. He doesn't look at Chains as he passes.

Nashville stops talking and watches as Stryker keeps going, having said nothing to anyone. He frowns at me, but I hold a hand up, letting him know it's okay.

"How much more are we going to get out of him?" I ask.

"Have you seen him?" he tilts his head at Chains. "Stryker got everything out of him. Storm was using him to get intel, he was probably promising him something in return he was never going to give."

"Some things never change, he was always a fucking snake, always out for what he could get for himself. Fucking waste," I look up at Chains.

"What do you want to do?" Nashville asks, looking through the door where Stryker disappeared.

"The only thing I can. Wake him up."

Razer brings a bucket of dirty water and throws it at Chains. He wakes up and thrashes but only long enough to remember how he is being kept upright and he cries out, some garbled shit coming through his broken teeth.

Everything about him is defeated. Deep down inside, I feel that too. No one ever wants to do this to someone they've called a brother for years. It's the only way to deal with traitors. I've learned a hard lesson with Storm. Its ironic Chains is the one paying for that mistake.

He has one good eye that he manages to open as Razer steps up and hands me a gun. This is the side of myself that is inevitable given the life I grew up in. As he stares at me, a drop of moisture squeezing from his eye. I have to harden my heart and forget everything going on.

This is who I am and nothing I do is going to change that. I point the gun at his head and fire. There is no point dragging it out, monologuing over why he did what he did and what it means to betray his family. Stryker will have made him see that.

His head jerks and then drops forward. My eyes squeeze shut for the briefest of moments, then I turn and hand the gun to Razer.

"Stryker stays out of this."

Nashville nods and turns to Chains. Him and Razer now have the job of getting him off those hooks and over to the pigs.

The night sky seems much brighter all the way out here, stars scattered across the inky blackness lighting the way as I head back to my bike.

This whole mess is fucked, and I hate what I had to do but it's done and it's time to move on.

One problem down, two more to go.

Why do I get the feeling none of this is going to go away as easily as we hope?

I spend the rest of the night at the clubhouse, trying to sleep but thinking about shit from the past. How close Storm was to my dad all those years ago. My father never made it to officer status at the club, but he was well liked, loyal, if somewhat stupid at times. Accidentally shooting himself while cleaning a gun was the way he was always going to die.

Him and Storm were often together, he would have been pissed at what his old friend did, getting thrown out of the MC. Never thought I'd wish the old bastard was still around so I could get some advice on the fucking bastard threatening the club.

At least now I know what we're up against, and how damn serious they are. Me and half of my officers could have been wiped out in one night. They've gone to ground since their plan fell through, and they must know Chains is off the map too by now.

At least their way inside the club is taken care of. Now we need to find them.

Back at the house a couple of days later, Jesse says he has work to catch up on so I need to stay with Oscar. He looks a little pale with dark circles under his eyes, but when I ask about it he waves me off. He reminds me Oscar isn't sleeping great, his nightmares seem to be getting worse.

This is all I need. How the hell do I get help for my son when no one is supposed to know he is here. Sheridan hasn't picked up the last few times I've called her. It's been a while since she checked on Oscar.

She's an okay mom to our son, her showing up for me to look after him while she took a break wasn't totally out of character. I've never had reason to doubt her when it came to him, but she had problems in the past with drugs and bad choices.

Making sure Oscar is okay, I text Speedway to come inside.

"Hey, what's up?" he asks as he comes into the kitchen, he looks through the arch at Oscar and waves at him.

"You heard from Sheridan?"

"Not for a while, why?"

"She hasn't been checking in."

His lips go down in thought. "Shit, do you think she's using?"

"You know her better than me," I grab a glass and fill it with water.

"I mean," he slides onto a stool and looks at his hands. "She's been a little distant lately, but I didn't think it was down to that."

"She has not ignored him this long before." I look in on Oscar playing with his puppy.

"You think she's in trouble?" His head comes up fast. "With everything going on?"

"Don't jump to conclusions," I reassure him. "No one knows about her ties to me. Try to get hold of her. If you know where she's gone head there."

"What about watching out for Oscar?"

"I'll get another brother here."

"You'll have to tell them about him," he looks at my son again.

I've already thought about that. Jesse spends that much time with him, and at my place, no one would think he wasn't his father. The thought of that makes my heart pound, but it's for his safety. I can't lose sight of that.

Speedway agrees to go check on his sister and I call Rebel about getting someone else over here, then I fire off a text to let Jesse know. I watch Oscar playing and wonder what it must be like, to be able to take your child out, something as simple as getting ice cream.

I never would have chosen to bring a kid into the world, my world, if I could have helped it. My thoughts turn to Taylor. If I'm going to keep fucking her, I need to make sure she's on the pill. Condoms break. Making that mistake again isn't an option. Nor is putting Taylor in danger.

Another few days pass with us getting nowhere on finding Storm. The guy Juice followed after their attempted mass execution of my men, has vanished too. I've no idea how long he is going to stay underground or what he will plan next.

It's fucking pissing me off.

After putting Oscar to bed and sending Jesse home, I sit down with a beer and look around my house. This place cost me a fortune, it's in a good neighborhood and Oscar is safe here. I've done everything I can to make sure nothing can happen to my family in this house.

The second beer is going down nicely when I get a text telling me to check the link. I open it up and read through how the police have found and arrested six students from one of the most prestigious universities in the state. They're under suspicion of being those responsible for the motorcycle attacks.

I call Blaze when I'm done.

"The news is a little behind, two of them were released on bail this morning. He wasn't picked up. Lots of texts back and forth since. Its pretty fucked up, but it worked."

He's keeping things as cryptic as possible over the phone. "Keep an eye on it. I don't want them taking what I'm owed."

"The two that got out concern me, I've got Ronin on them."

"Okay, give it a couple more days, then we do it."

I set the phone down, but it rings before I have a chance to think.

It's Taylor, for a second I pause, I haven't contacted her since the night everything went down with Chains. It felt wrong to go to her after that. She'll be calling because she's seen the news. The idea of her thanking me when she has no clue what my next steps are isn't sitting right.

Blowing out a heavy breath I hover my finger over decline, then slide it the other way, cursing myself for wanting a bit of her light in the darkness that is creeping over me lately.

"Hey," I answer, leaning back on the couch and picking up my beer.

"Hi. I wasn't sure whether to call."

"You can call me, Cherry. I might not always answer but I'll call you back." I mean that too, this isn't a lie. "It's been busy the last few days, but you caught me at home for once."

"I was calling about the news today. About the biker gang who attacked me. Was that you?"

"Don't sound so surprised, I told you I'd deal with it," I close my eyes.

"It did surprise me. I was expecting something else."

"Believe me, something else was on my mind. Getting them like this made better sense."

"Thank you."

"You don't need to thank me, Cherry. Fuckers deserved it after what they've been doing."

"I don't understand why they did it. They're all from affluent backgrounds, why would they want to do that kind of thing, it's not like they need the money."

"Some people are evil like that, looking for an excuse to hurt innocent people. They would have escalated. It really was only a matter of time. They were already getting worse when they hurt you."

"Then it's even better that you've stopped them."

"We'll see."

"What does that mean?"

"We need to make sure it sticks."

"Okay, well I wanted to say thank you. And..."

"And what?"

"Nothing, it's nothing."

"What aren't you saying, Cherry?"

I practically hear her swallow down her fears. "Do you want to come over?"

"You want me to come over?"

"I asked didn't I?" she says. "Let's not pretend this is easy."

"I'd love to, but I can't tonight."

"It's okay, I know your busy and... other things."

"It's not that," I say, wanting to laugh at her not being able to mention what we talked about the other night. "Oscar is in bed."

"Oh." She pauses, both of us remembering our first interaction and how I told her to forget she ever saw my son. "Noah, I didn't tell anybody. I mean, I had no reason to. I could have done cos I thought you were an ass when you got mad about it."

"I remember, Cherry."

Standing up, I walk to the kitchen counter and pick up the monitor. Oscar is fast asleep, poor kid was exhausted after I'd finished entertaining him. I've never had anyone around him before, but he should stay asleep. Or Speedway could come in and watch him while I go to her place.

But she has seen him, she knows about him. Shit...

"I understand."

"You could come here."

Her end goes silent, she's thinking about what it means that I'm asking her to come over when my son is here. I'm still trying to figure that out myself when she agrees.

"Be careful."

"Yes, I know."

I can see the eye roll in my mind's eye.

"See you soon, Cherry."

CHAPTER NINETEEN

Taylor

IT'S NOT LIKE I'M going to offer sex to thank him for having those assholes arrested. Even if they are already out on bail, it's impressive he got that far. And unexpected. I won't lie about that. I'm still shocked there weren't news stories about them being killed. Not that I would know, the guy had a helmet on, I couldn't identify him.

It's good that he did it this way, he didn't have to. When he said he was going to make him pay, this didn't seem like what he meant. What does it say about me that I'm disappointed about that.

And what does it say that I'm here, again, wanting to see this man who is dangerous and mysterious and really, really bad for me.

Dana will not be happy. Over the last few weeks since dad died, and the days after the attack, I've been thinking a lot about myself. How I've spent most of my life doing things to make other people happy.

As a nurse it's ingrained in me to take care of others, but I've always done the things my friends wanted to do, even when I wasn't in the mood.

Spending time with Noah makes *me* feel good and I want to get to know more about him. I should be scared of his motorcycle club but,

I'm not. He intrigues me. He thinks the same thing about me. He would not keep in touch, and definitely wouldn't let me come to the house while his baby is here.

The door opens and an embarrassing squeak comes from the back of my throat. Noah puts one arm up on the frame of the door and leans out. He isn't shirtless, but he is wearing a very tight white T-shirt that leaves nothing to the imagination, much like the black sweatpants.

"I've been watching you on the security camera for at least three minutes."

I put a hand over my mouth and try to hide the embarrassed smile.

"You coming in or do you want some more time to think about it?"

Noah doesn't have a chance to move when I duck under his arm and squeeze past. He closes and locks the door then turns and gives me of those looks of his. Like he is trying to decide what to do with me.

"What's that?" he points to my hands. I almost forgot I brought it.

"Cupcakes."

"You brought me cupcakes, Cherry?"

"I made too many and everyone at work told me stop bringing them in cos they're on diets and I didn't want them to go to waste so..."

He walks over and takes the box, lifting the lid and peering in. "They look professional. You sure you made them?"

I smack his arm, barely hard enough for him to feel it, and try to take the box. "I'll take them back home if you're going to insult me."

"No," he laughs, twisting so I can't get them. "I'm kidding. You brought them for me, so I'm going to eat them."

He goes around the counter, sets the box down and takes two out. My mouth goes dry as he peels the paper case off and licks the frosting. Could this man be any sexier? Seriously. I'm about to combust. Even though I came here determined to have more conversation with him and not fall into his bed.

Watching him eat the cake in three big bites makes that thought harder.

"They're good," he says. "You want?"

"I've eaten enough, they're for you... guys," I add at the end, my meaning clear.

"All that sugar will make my life a million times harder if Oscar eats more than half a cake." He eats another one.

"If there are any left," I laugh.

"They're tasty." He grins at me. He looks down and finally notices. "You got your bandage off."

"It was just a sprain and needed some support. It's good now."

"Hmm, that is good." Why do I get the impression he isn't meaning it for medical purposes? "Want a beer?"

"Beer and cupcakes. It's like being back in college."

Noah laughs, grabs everything and we head through the archway into a less formal sitting room than the one he took me to the other night. We sit close together on the couch and Noah eats another cake.

"I don't know about your son being hyper. You've eaten three of those."

"Dinner was leftover takeout, I'm hungry."

He eyes me when he says that and it almost makes my resolve not to jump him vanish into a puff of smoke, but I hold off.

"Your son, he's sleeping?" Noah's jaw clenches. "I'm sorry, I'm curious."

"About why I don't want anyone to know about him?"

"More like his name," I duck my head a little. "How old he is."

"Oscar and he's two."

The tension isn't leaving his shoulders. We need a change of subject. Given what he does for a living... Wait, is being the President of a motorcycle club a job? Does he get paid? Shit, I don't want to know the answer to how they make their money.

"It's a touchy subject for me." He's staring at his beer bottle as he continues and I keep quiet. "I never thought I'd have kids or wanted them if I'm being honest. An accident happened and nine months later, she told me."

"You didn't know?"

"Not until he was born, but she did the right thing telling me. It was a shock, won't lie, but I can't imagine my life without him now."

He glances to the side, and I follow his gaze to a baby monitor. My heart melts a little.

"You want to ask about his mom, right?"

"I wasn't going to."

"You're a bad liar, Cherry."

"I never said I didn't want to know, I said I wasn't going to ask."

"We have joint custody. She's away right now," he frowns. "We split his time so we both see him equally."

That is surprisingly normal given his lifestyle. Getting my hopes up is still premature. "And Jesse takes care of him when you're busy?"

"Yeah, he loves Uncle Jesse. Sometimes..." the smile that started fades. "It feels like he spends more time with him than I do. With the way things are, it's difficult. I try to be there as much as I can."

"He seemed happy when I came around. Even if I did think you were a jackass. The kid gave you a slap on my behalf."

"Is that right?" He smirks at me.

"He's obviously smart, he could tell you were being rude."

He rolls his eyes. "Fuck, you're gonna make me say it."

"It's a little late."

"Yeah well, I have my reasons. But, shit, sorry for being a jackass."

He holds in his laugh for five seconds, which gets harder when I nudge him. Noah pokes me in the ribs making me shriek, then slap a hand over my mouth and look up.

"He's a heavy sleeper, you don't have to worry about making noise. Within reason. Although making you scream is fast becoming one of my favorite things to do."

My resolve ran right out the door without a second look back. Noah grabs my hip and pulls me toward him and I don't fight it, straddling his lap. He sets my beer bottle down on the table beside him, then brings his hands to my hips.

"I'm really tempted to go get some cupcakes so I can lick frosting off your tits," he says, his hand gliding up to cup them. My back arches, pushing them further into his palms. "But that would mean getting up and I don't want to do that."

"I'm sweet enough," I murmur.

"Fucking right."

Noah wastes no time taking off my shirt and unclasping my bra. His lips are on one breast and his hand on the other in seconds, and I clamp my teeth onto my lower lip to keep from crying out. As much as I love the attention he is lavishing on them, I want to kiss him, so grab his face and lift it. Any protest dies as my mouth fuses to his, and he gives back as good as he's getting, his hands sliding around to unbutton my jeans.

He tilts and lowers me onto the couch and drags them off, pausing to stare at me a moment. I want to ask him what he's thinking, at the same time I don't want to break the moment. Noah does that all by himself when he grips the side of my panties with both hands and rips them.

I gasp as the fabric tears and he pushes it aside, gliding his fingers around and spearing them inside me. I'm wet enough from his kisses but the shock of it has me arching up, and he takes full advantage, grabbing a handful of my hair and biting my nipple.

His fingers scissor inside of me and he places his mouth over mine to swallow the moans, shifting at the same time to push his sweatpants out of the way and get up on the couch. Pushing my legs apart he lays over me.

"Fuck," he groans. His face is conflicted and I don't understand why he's stopped.

"Are you on birth control?" he growls out.

"Yes." I answer straight away and stare at him.

"I don't have any condoms down here and I can't wait to get inside of you."

It's reckless for so many reasons, but I nod, and forget all of them when he starts to push inside me.

"Oh fuck," he groans as he slips in. "That feels so good, I feel every part of you, so tight and fucking wet."

His thrusts are shallow at first as he gets used to it. I almost ask him if we should stop, remember all the reasons why this is a bad idea, but he starts to push in deeper and grabs hold of my thigh, curling it around his hip, as his mouth comes down on mine.

"What the fuck are you doing to me, Cherry?" He whispers against my mouth before stroking his tongue back inside, tangling slowly with mine.

I don't know, I want to say, because I am confused too. The words stay trapped inside of me. It has to be because he is inside of me, moving slowly, every thrust punctuated by a grunt and his tongue rolling around mine.

Noah runs his hand through my hair as he kisses a path down my chin and jaw, along the column of my neck. His thrusts get deeper and he is groaning too, blowing out deep breaths in rhythm with his thrusts. My head tips back as the feel of his bare cock dragging back and forth makes everything in me tighten, I feel it coming, same as him as he pulls his head up to watch me.

I tilt my hips to match his thrusts and grip his arms as I start to come.

"Jesus," Noah's face scrunches as I squeeze around him and he groans when I let go, my eyes squeezing tight. They open abruptly as he pulls out of me and grabs his cock, his hand moving fast over it, his eyes between my legs.

I can't help but watch in fascination as he comes, and it hits my stomach. He was right to do it, but I'm disappointed. Except seeing his whole body all locked up, his biceps bulging, and his abdomen tight as he comes makes up for it.

He's beautiful and I'm in so much trouble because I don't want this to end.

His chest is heaving as his head falls forward and he opens his eyes to look at me. He stares, and it feels a lot like he owns me, every part of my body. And more.

"Shit, Cherry," he sighs, catching his breath. "That was hot," he grins. "I made a mess of you."

All I can do is nod. He rolls up and gets off me, then holds out a hand and helps me to my feet. "Let's go clean you up."

He grabs the baby monitor and we head upstairs. This time, he gets in the shower washing his cum off me. Then he lowers onto his knees and does what is fast becoming one of my favorite things, driving me to the edge of insanity all over again. When we get out and are drying off, I pull his towel away and lower to my knees.

"Hmm," he cups the back of my head as I swallow his cock down my throat and he thrusts into me. "Seeing your lips wrapped around my cock is never going to get old, Cherry. Fuck, yeah. You're gonna let me fuck that throat and take it all, Cherry. Everything."

I nod and he thrusts even harder, getting a grip of my hair as he moves in and out and I do what he says, reveling in the praise he gives me as I swallow every last drop. He leans against the counter as I get to my feet, his eyes on me.

"You might have broken me," he smirks at me.

"I hope not," I give him a cheeky wink and walk out of the bathroom to the sound of his amused laughter.

What happens now? Noah comes up behind me and presses into my back. He's naked and firm and I melt back against him. He doesn't say anything as he kisses my neck, then walks around me to pull the covers back. When he nudges me, I go willingly and we get into the bed together.

It's not the first time he's slept beside me, but this feels different. So much more. And after what we did downstairs, the trust we both placed in each other...

"Go to sleep, Cherry," he kisses my temple and then rolls onto his back and flicks off the lamp.

I'm still awake long after he drifts off. Falling for someone this fast is so out of character for me, but Noah isn't like anyone I've ever met before. There are two sides to him, one I've seen a little of, and one he is slowly letting me become a part of.

At some point things will change and I'll get hurt. It's too late to stop it. Eventually, I'm going to have to figure out how to deal with that, for now, I let it go and roll onto my side, shuffling closer. Noah lifts his arm and I move closer, placing my head on his chest.

I'm not sure he woke up, but if this is all he can give me. I'll take it.

Chapter Twenty

Nero

THE CRACKLE OF THE baby monitor and Oscar's cries startle me out of sleep. He's thrashing around in his crib. Taylor moves back and makes a surprised noise as I jump out of bed and grab my pants, tugging them on as I run down the hall.

He's screaming and rolling from side to side his hands up in the air. "Fuck," I rush over and try to lift him but he starts batting at me. What the hell? My heart is thrashing in my chest as he rolls over, his eyes are half open, but he isn't awake.

"Noah."

"Not now," I try to reach him again.

Taylor grabs my arm and pulls me, I almost lash out at her but stop myself as she drags me backward.

"He's having a night terror," she takes my face and tries to turn it, but I can't stop looking at Oscar as he cries and shouts. "You have to let him come out of it on his own."

"What the fuck are talking about?" I snap at her.

She doesn't shrink away keeping tight hold of me. "He won't recognize you, he isn't awake and if you try to bring him out of it, he will not let you comfort him, he'll fight you because he won't know who you are."

I'm still desperate to get to him but her words sink in. She's right, that is what happens. Even Jesse says Oscar fights him when he tries to wake him up. I look down at her. "Night terrors?"

"Yes, my friend's daughter has them. They're normal in kids this age."

"There is nothing normal about that," I cry out, watching Oscar.

"Just give it a moment, Noah, trust me."

I want to, but fuck. I drop down on my knees beside the crib, Taylor lowers with me, still holding my arm.

"He will need you when he wakes up."

"This is fucking impossible," I force the words out past all the emotion ripping through my chest.

"He's soothing himself, Noah, he'll wake up soon."

She's right, the thrashing has stopped, his cries are becoming less out of terror and more out of upset. He rolls over and his eyes open. Taylor finally lets me go and leans back.

"Dada."

"Jesus," I stumble over my own feet to get up and lift him out of the crib. He's crying more in his usual way now and he clings on to me. I press my lips to the top of his head and hold him tight, whispering that he is okay.

In my peripheral I see Taylor getting up. Sometimes I forget she is a nurse, but kids aren't her specialty as far as I know.

My heart is still thrashing, the adrenalin taking longer to wear off than it is for Oscar. He's settled against me, his face snuffling against my chest.

"Does he have a favorite comforter or bear?" she asks.

I nod and bend down to pick up Oscar Two. The little shit of a puppy has replaced his other favorite bear. Oscar instantly reaches for it.

"Read him a story, reassure him but you have to let him sleep."

Usually I'd bring him to my bed, with her here, that's not possible. But I don't have to leave him. She walks out before I have a chance to say anything. We go over to the chair where I used to feed him, and I lift the blanket, sitting down and wrapping it around us. The book he loves is within reach so I grab that.

As I read, he makes little noises, sometimes he says the words but after a while, his eyes drift shut again. I keep reading until I know he's asleep, carefully setting the book down.

Fuck that was one of the scariest moments I've ever experienced. The shit I've done in my life and this is what nearly broke me.

If it was safe I'd hold him like this all night but the risk of falling asleep and dropping him scares me more than not holding him. He goes down in the crib and rolls over without a care in the world and I lean over and stroke his hair.

It's going to take me a long time to get those images out of my head. Sitting down beside the crib, I watch him, no idea how much time goes by.

When I'm sure he is okay, I get up and head back down to my room. Taylor is in my bed and I stand in the doorway and watch her. If she wasn't here tonight, I could have made everything worse.

How do I not know how to deal with this? What kind of father am I? My phone is on the night stand so I sit and pick it up, searching for night terrors. Everything Taylor told me to do is the right way to deal with this. If anyone else had told me how to take care of my son, I would have told them to get the fuck out.

"Is he okay?" Taylor rolls over and her hand touches my back.

"Sleeping."

After a beat, she asks, "do you want me to go?"

"No," I set the phone down and turn around to her. She is still wearing one of my T-shirts which she must have grabbed when she followed me to Oscar's room. "Everything you said... If you weren't here."

"You would have dealt with it," she reassures me. "You're his dad, he would have eventually come out of it."

"You said he wouldn't recognize me."

"He would have, he knows your scent, your voice and that you bring him comfort. It might have taken longer than normal but you wouldn't have hurt him, Noah."

How the fuck she knew those are my thoughts... I shake my head, not that I don't agree with her, she's right. She's amazing. She slides back as I get into the bed but I move toward her, dragging her into my side.

There are no more words, just emotions I'm not used to. Her hand gently strokes over my chest and after a moment, I take it in mine and hold it still over my heart, which eventually slows to a normal beat.

Sleep is a long time coming and I spend most of it staring down at her. It might be wrong to let her get under my skin but it's too late to stop it. And I don't know what the fuck to do with that.

She finds us downstairs in the morning, hovering in the doorway in my T-shirt and a pair of my shorts. I'm hardly going to complain about it, given her clothes are in the corner down here.

Oscar looks over at her. "Who dat?" he asks.

I can't help the smile. "This is my friend, Ch.. Taylor." I correct myself and wink at her. "Taylor this Oscar."

Those words sound really fucking foreign but Taylor comes over and crouches down, reaching out a hand. Oscar stares at it, then lifts his and she gently shakes.

"Nice to meet you, Oscar. And who is this?"

"Oscar Two."

"His name is Oscar as well.

"Oscar Two," he repeats.

"As in Oscar number two," I explain. Taylor smiles and nods.

"Have you had breakfast?" she asks and I shake my head.

I've been too busy practically smothering him, to the point he told me to back off. That made me laugh. He's been listening to me and Jesse too much. "I'll make some pancakes," I start to get up.

Taylor tells me not to, to stay with Oscar while she makes them. Something about this is oddly welcome, but foreign too. She heads off to the kitchen and starts looking for the things she needs. What should be happening is me telling her to go, instead I make sure Oscar is okay and walk into the kitchen.

"I'll leave when they're ready," she says. "I needed to get my clothes."

"Stay," I say, surprising myself as much as her. "Have breakfast with us."

"Are you sure?"

"Positive," I glance back, then take her panties out of my pocket. "You're going to need to borrow a pair of m boxers."

Her cheeks flush when she sees the torn fabric. When we came into the room this morning, I set him down and gathered up our discarded clothes, finding her shredded panties and shoving them in my pocket.

"I don't need to do that," she says.

"The thought of you wearing a pair of my underwear is kind of hot."

Taylor stares at me then shakes her head like I'm crazy. Maybe I am but something about her in my clothes is making me fucking crazy. Our stare off is interrupted by a little body grabbing my leg and holding up his arms.

"Hungry dada."

"Taylor is making some pancakes for us," I lift him up and hold him.

"Mmm pancakes."

"You like pancakes?" Taylor asks him as she pours batter into the pan. "My dad used to make me pancakes when I was little. But he did this really special thing."

She grabs some fruit from the fridge. Jesse's doing. As the batter starts to firm, she drops two blueberries in for eyes, then uses the end of a spoon to make a mouth. It's cooking fast enough that the batter doesn't spill back into space.

"A smiley," Oscar laughs.

My eyes are locked on her as she makes happy pancakes for my son. And I sit back after setting him in his high chair and she makes a smaller pancake for Oscar Two, which has Oscar so happy it's like last night never happened. While Oscar rips into the pancake, I walk over and wrap an arm around her waist.

"Do I get a happy pancake?" I arch a brow.

"If you give me coffee," she taps my shoulder with the spatula.

"Think I can manage that." While Oscar is distracted, I cup her chin and press a kiss to her lips.

If my brothers could see me now, I know exactly what they'd say. It starts with P and ends with whipped.

Fuck if I don't care.

While she makes more food, and Oscar has spent most of his time chatting away to Taylor, I call Jesse to check on him and whether he is okay to come over. He agrees, sounding better than he looked. Shit if he has been dealing with these night terrors and not telling me, I'm going to break his arm.

We eat together and I go get dressed then come back to find Taylor rolling a ball for the puppy and Oscar bounces along after it, pretending to fetch.

She looks up at me and instinctively knows. She tells Oscar she needs to go, and he pouts asking when she is coming back.

"Soon buddy," I tell him. "Uncle Jesse is on his way."

"Yay!" he shouts. "Bye Taylor."

"Bye Oscar," she grins as she comes over. "So fickle."

"Uncle Jesse is his favorite," I sigh. She cocks her head but doesn't comment.

She is already dressed, and I did make her put on a pair of my underwear and told her I was keeping hers. Her response was so long as I don't wear hers, which made me snort and tell her that shit will *never* happen.

We go to the front door and finally, fucking finally I get to put my hands on her. She falls against me easily as I press her into the wall and kiss her, my tongue touching hers until she is panting and my hand has slid up to grab her tit.

The door opens and Jesse stands there, staring at us. Taylor shifts back and my hand drops but I don't step away from her, just stare at him. He knew I had her checked out, and he wasn't happy about that. He is even more surprised when a little rocket comes hurtling towards him.

He picks Oscar up and looks from me to Taylor, knowing I've let her around my son says more than words ever can.

"Good to see you, Taylor," he tells her and moves past us.

"Oh shit," she whispers, watching after him.

"It's fine," I kiss her again, less like I'm fucking her mouth and more like I'm saying goodbye and don't want to. "I'll explain to him."

Her expression says she wants me to explain it to her too, but I put a hand on her back and guide her to the door. Can't explain what you don't fucking understand. Once she's in her car and pulling away I head back inside.

Jesse has set Oscar up with the plastic laptop he is convinced will teach him to read even though it doesn't have a real screen, just letters on the fake keys. It makes fucking irritating noises too, and was hidden at the bottom of the toy box. Who knew he could be a petty little fucker?

"Are you out of your mind?" he asks coming into the kitchen.

"It's not what you think?"

"Having your hand on my nurse's boob and your tongue down her throat is not what I think," he widens his eyes. "She stayed the night?"

"Boob?"

"Fuck off, *Nero*."

Point well and truly fucking taken. "She's different," I tell him.

"Of course she's different, she isn't one of your club girls, or the strippers and women who want to fuck you because of the patch you wear."

"You done insulting me?"

"Noah, Jesus. She's my nurse."

"You think I don't know that. You're the one who brought her here."

"Don't put this on me," he shakes his head. "What is it? You getting what you want out of it."

"She met Oscar."

"What does that mean? You don't know do you? You don't know how to handle it, but you don't want to stop. Have you even thought about her. About who you are."

"She knows Jesse."

He stops ranting at me and his brow furrows. I explain everything that's happened over the last few weeks and how this isn't something either one of us were planning. He's shocked she was attacked and mentions the arrests, eyeing me but not asking anything else about that.

"So she knows what you do, about your son, what happens next? What are you getting out of this, besides sex," he adds eyeing me.

"Like you said, I can't explain it."

"Oh *shit*, you have feelings for her?"

"Shit." We both turn to Oscar who is standing behind us. "Shit," he repeats.

"Fuck," I groan.

"Fuck," Oscar says. I smother a laugh as Jesse admonishes my two-year-old for saying grown up words. "Fuck, shit," he repeats.

My laugh gets harder and Jesse kicks me. Oscar is laughing now too and Jesse is trying real hard to be strict.

At least he's taken the focus off me and Taylor. Kid deserves to say a couple of bad words for that assist.

Chapter Twenty One

Nero

It's been three weeks since the arrests and two of them have been charged, the other three have had their rich parents get them off. Guess the two scholarship kids are taking the fall. I'll deal with them when the time comes but for now, Morris, the shitbag who laid his hands on Taylor is about to find out what happens when he messes with what's mine.

Taylor has spent a lot of time over at my house. Oscar has taken to her like she's his new best friend and she is good with him. With her help, we're getting a better handle on the night terrors, which I spoke to a doctor about, and he confirmed Taylor's advice.

They haven't gone away, and the doctor wasn't very reassuring when he said they can last a few years, but he did say it was nothing specific that causes them. He doesn't know my fucking lifestyle, but he said night terrors are not the same as nightmares.

Mostly they're unexplainable and go away on their own. The only time I need to be concerned is if they're becoming more frequent and harder for him to come out of.

Jesse is coming around to the fact his nurse is in my bed at least three times a week. Mostly because when she is there, I'm there, so Oscar is seeing a lot more of me. He's said for a while that is what we both need.

I'm getting attached and even though it scares the shit out of me for what it could mean to her, I can't walk away. This woman has me in a chokehold.

And when we fuck, which we do a lot, it's like I'm in goddamn heaven. I've never gone back to a woman as many times as I have to Taylor. Not only in bed, but talking, interacting, learning about her life, having her be a part of my son's. It's fucking insane, but I don't want to lose it. Because I'm a selfish motherfucker.

Speedway hasn't been able to track down Sheridan, which is worrying me. I've sent another brother down to Alexandria where she is supposed to be staying with a friend with him to track her down. Blaze confirmed her phone is switched off.

I'm not convinced this is Storm, he's too lazy and wouldn't follow her down there to get to me. He doesn't know about her and Oscar, anyway.

We've been planning how to take down Morris when Ronin pops his head in after knocking and lets me know there is a woman in the bar asking for me. I pull out my phone and check it. There are a couple of messages from Taylor saying she needs to talk to me. She wouldn't come here though.

"We grab him tomorrow," I tell them. "Figure out where he'll be and get the farm ready."

They watch me walk out and I know exactly what they're thinking but I don't care. Taylor will get a lot of attention in the bar. The majority of my guys know not to mess around with women who are linked to anyone, but at the same time there is this fucking shitty rule that unless a woman is claimed, she's free game.

Anyone fucking looks at her sideways, I'll snap their necks.

She's sitting at the bar talking to Raven when I come in through the back. Some of the brothers are looking her way but they've also made it clear they're interested in Raven. Rebel is almost as bad as me when it comes to his sister, he'd cut off their balls before they got them anywhere near his sisters pussy.

Raven looks up as I move through the bar, her brow arched. Fuck, she saw me eating Taylor out on her bar that first time she showed up here.

There is something more to the look now, a shrewdness. Not in a bad way, in a way that tells me she is going to give me shit for having a woman come back for more.

"Hey," I lean against the bar and Taylor turns to me. "What are you doing here?"

"I was at home and wanted to see you," she shrugs. "Somewhere other than at your house."

"Oh, girl," Raven smirks. "Get it."

"Stay out of this," I tell her without taking my eyes off Taylor.

She laughs as she walks to the other end of the bar. There are eyes on us as I take a step closer to Taylor. She's watching every move I make, as I study every nuance of her face. I've held off on this because I'm still in two minds about bringing her in.

What I am coming to realize is, she's already in. I'm planning on killing the asshole who hurt her tomorrow night. She can never know about that but it's getting harder to hide her away. It's bad enough hiding Oscar from everyone.

I hear more people coming in through the back and know it has to be my officers. The other brothers use the front door. I feel their eyes on me, they're waiting to see what I'm going to do. Rebel is the only who knows anything about her. Somehow the rest of them have got wind of it.

"Do you know what you're doing?" I ask her. "What you're getting into with me?"

"I've spent the last month and a half learning all about you, Noah," she touches my cut. "Just not everything."

"It's different here."

"You've told me that."

"You're feeling bold tonight."

"Something like that" she looks over her shoulder and back at me. "They're all watching."

"That's because no woman has ever made me walk out of a meeting when I hear she's in the bar looking for me. Only women who get treatment like that are old ladies."

Her eyes widen and she takes in a breath.

"I'm not sure you're ready for that, Cherry."

"Since I got here, I've heard three women ask where you are."

"Only three?"

She pokes me in the stomach. "I'll let that go because I trust you, Noah."

That makes my heart pound and for once, I'm not scared by it. I'm still me though and she needs to remember that. "Good," I lean closer to her ear. "Because the only woman I want wrapped around my cock, is you."

"It goes both ways, doesn't it? When you claim someone?" she asks after regaining her composure.

"Who has been filling your head?"

"I'm smart enough to figure these things out for myself."

"You are," I take a lock of her hair and wrap it around my fingers. "You really want me to claim you, Cherry. In front of everyone in here?"

"Would I be here if I didn't?"

"You don't know what it means, Cherry. What tying yourself to me is going to be like."

This isn't a conversation we should be having in here, but she is determined and I fucking want her. It's not the right time, with everything going on at the club.

All of these thoughts are warring inside my head as she watches me. Something like disappointment starts to creep into her eyes.

Fuck it.

I grab the back of her head and kiss her. I'm not sure if the noise dies down or gets louder because Taylor grips my cut and kisses me back, rising up on the stool to get closer to me. There is no going back now. This isn't me making her an old lady, we need to talk about that more but I'm making a statement as I grab her legs and wrap them around my hips.

The eyes of most of the people in here, the ones who understand, are on us as I walk to the back of the bar with her wrapped around me. I hold her under her ass with one arm and the back of her head with the other so I can keep kissing her.

"Fuck, I think I just got pregnant," I hear someone say.

Taylor laughs against my lips, because it wasn't a woman who said that. I don't set her down until we're in one of the bedrooms. One that looks like the sheets have been changed and smells clean. I lock the door then walk to the bed and drop her on it. She sits back and looks up, her head tilted back.

"I want to know everything about you, every side of you. I'm not scared."

"You should be," I lightly stroke her jaw then grab her chin. "I'm a scary man, Cherry."

"I don't care."

"Don't say that. You should care, because there are going to be times when you want to ask me questions that I will never answer. If this is what you really want, you have to go into it knowing that, Taylor," I use her real name so she understands this is important.

"I've seen you around Oscar, and Jesse, the life you live outside of this club. I know you're a good man Noah."

"One who does bad things."

She reaches up and touches my chest. My breath catches as she draws up my shirt and presses her palm to my skin. "It's all a part of you. Nero, Noah, they're the same person. We all have different sides to us. I want both sides of you."

There is still a lot I should say but the words get stuck in my throat. Instead I push her head further back and lean down to kiss her. There are times when I've been rough during sex but nothing that would ever hurt her. I still have no intention of doing that but here, I am Nero.

I grab her hips and roughly turn her over so she is face down, her legs are over the edge, her knees almost touching the floor. She doesn't do anything to stop me when I push her skirt up and drag her panties down her legs, or at the sound of my belt unbuckling.

All she does is hold on as I drag her hips up so her toes are on the floor and fuck into her, hard enough that the bed shakes. She lets out a moan then a surprised yelp when I smack her ass cheek.

"Do you still want to know this side of me?" I grunt, thrusting into her again hard enough to punctuate the question. "Do you, Cherry? You think you can handle this?" I slap her other ass cheek and she moans louder this time.

"Yes."

My eyes close as I swivel my hips, giving her a little reprieve from the hardness.

"Then hold on tight, Cherry."

She grips the sheets as I fuck her harder than I have before, slapping her ass and pulling her hair. Never hard enough to really hurt, only hard enough to have her moaning and clutching out and her cunt gripping me hard enough to make my cock swell and pulse. I reach around and pinch her clit, I may be a selfish bastard right now but I will never leave her wanting.

My cum pulses into her and she lets out a scream I'm sure the brothers can hear but all that does is make me possessive, wanting them to know I own this woman. And she fucking owns me.

I take a chance and give her a ride home, Nashville follows at a distance and he will hang around after I've left her to make sure she's safe. But after that claiming, I need her at my back, to make it known in a way they can actually see, that she is mine. No man in the MC can deny when a woman rides at a man's back, she is off limits.

Taylor is anxious and makes little scared noises but when we get back to her house, her cheeks are rosy and her eyes full of excitement. I help her off the bike and take the helmet. She stares at me but I won't kiss her, not out here.

Instead I run a hand up her thigh, under her skirt. "Don't take a shower till tomorrow."

She frowns.

"I want to know my cum is still inside this pussy when I can't be," I press her panties into the slit, forcing the fabric inside. They're still wet and my dick starts to get hard again, but she needs to wrap her head around what happened. "What are you going to do, Cherry?"

"Keep your cum inside me," she lifts a brow.

"Fucking hell," I shake my head with a laugh. "Get inside, lock up. I'll call you."

She does as I ask and I nod to Nashville as I drive down the block where he is waiting. He'll make sure it's safe before he leaves.

Rebel is waiting for me in the big room when I get back.

"Now that we're done with the claiming, can we get back to business?"

"It wasn't planned, but fuck you," I drawl.

"Yeah, yeah. I think you're fucking crazy but when do you ever listen to me."

"That's bullshit and you know it. Where she's concerned, I don't need to listen to anyone. Make sure she's safe," I add. There is no need to say what that means. The whole club will watch out for her now. Whether she knows it or not, she's part of us.

Chapter Twenty Two

Taylor

"You haven't stopped smiling for over a week now." I turn to face Shannon. She is leaning in my doorway eyeing me. "You either won the lottery or you're getting laid."

"Shannon," my mouth drops open. "You can't say that."

"I just did, and you confirmed. Who is the lucky guy?"

I haven't thought about how I'm going to explain Noah to people. Dana knows, and she was shocked as hell when I told her what happened a couple of nights ago. She wants to meet him properly now and denied having an ulterior motive to meet Stryker. Noah hasn't introduced me to everyone yet but I've met Nashville a couple of times now.

"He is a friend of a patient," I tell her sheepishly.

"Which patient?" her smile fades.

"Jesse Cartwright."

"Well, if he looks anything like him," she sighs and straightens up. "It's my duty as your manager and administrator for this clinic that under no circumstances should you have any kind of relationship with a patient."

"I think Noah would agree."

She snorts a laugh. "Just keep it professional here. Or we can hand him off to Caitlyn."

"No don't worry, I know how to uphold my oath, Shannon. I barely see him."

That's true enough, when Noah is at home it gives Jesse time to himself, to get back to work. When I do see him, I try not to think of him as a patient.

"He isn't due for a follow up for four months."

She nods, then comes in and closes the door, sitting down opposite me. I'm not sure what this is about until she gets the face she used to make when dad first got ill.

"How are you doing?" she asks. "With everything."

"I'm good Shannon. You don't need to worry about me. I'm not going to lie and say I've moved on and don't think about him. I still don't go a day without thinking of him."

"This guy is making it less difficult. Does he know?"

"Yeah, we've talked about it. Shannon, trust me, I'm fine."

"I'm glad, honey. It's nice to see the old you back."

Her words stay on my mind as the day goes on. Noah isn't making me forget, he's making me cope with it better. Seeing him with Oscar makes me happy. He still thinks he isn't being the best father he can, but he doesn't see what I do.

My mind takes a sharp left turn to the other night. It didn't matter to me that he was trying to show the different side of him. As far as I am concerned Noah doesn't have two sides, there is no good and bad, he's just him. Maybe that makes me a fool or people will think I'm blind to what he does but the part of him that cares for Oscar, for me, hasn't dulled.

After my shift Noah texts when I get in the car.

Noah: Want to come over tonight?

Taylor: Over what?

Noah: You're a dirty girl

Taylor: You bring it out in me. And yes. I'll go straight there if that is okay?

Noah: I'll let Jesse know

Taylor: Did you talk to him?

Noah: Don't worry about him Cherry. He likes you, and he loves me

Taylor: I'm worried he doesn't like us together

Noah: He's coming around. GTG

There won't be any more texts. The whole GTG is him signing off.

Jesse's car is outside when I arrive, and although Noah hasn't come right out and said someone is watching the house, I see the same guy who has been there every time I come over.

Jesse opens the door and welcomes me inside. We've always had a good relationship before now so I hate that he is looking at me differently.

"I've made dinner," he says. "Lasagna."

"Smells great."

"It's Oscar's favorite."

"Can I help?"

"Most of it's done but you can help with getting us some bread."

We work together in silence, the only noise is Oscar playing in the other room. He greeted me when I first came in but his little baby laptop has him fully occupied.

There is still no sign of Noah after we've eaten and Jesse tells me not to overthink it. Sometimes this happens, and he doesn't get home when he says he is going to.

"I know you have your concerns about me and Noah," I say, after I've cleaned up Oscar's face and put him down. He runs over to get his puppy and starts pretending it's real.

"You have to know what you're getting yourself into."

"Thank you, and I do," I lean forward on my stool. "You see the good in him too Jesse."

"You really don't know the bad. How he gets sometimes."

"I can handle it."

He rubs his forehead and sighs. His skin looks a little clammy.

"Have you had your insulin today?"

"Of course, you know I take it properly, Taylor."

"Jesse, you're sweating."

"Don't be a *nurse* with me," he gives me a smirk.

"Where is your glucometer? Are you having any abdominal pain, or feeling nausea?"

"Taylor, I'm fine. I'll grab some juice."

"I'll get it, you get your kit."

Noah keeps a steady supply of the juice Jesse needs. When I come back after grabbing the juice, he wobbles a little almost spilling the juice. Jesus, I help him onto a stool and hold up the glass. I don't like his color and he's getting more disoriented. With long practiced efficiency, I take out the glucometer, set it up with a test strip and quickly wash my hands, checking in on Oscar. No child needs to see this.

"He's used to it," Jesse says.

He closes his eyes as he swallows some juice and stays that way. He doesn't even flinch when I gently prick the side of his fingertip until a small bead of blood comes out then move it onto the test strip. I use an alcohol wipe to clean his hand as the glucometer starts to work.

I keep an eye on him then glance back at the glucometer. "Shit."

"What?"

"It's at sixty-four." I stare at the screen. This can't be right. His blood sugar is way below seventy and he could go into hypoglycemic shock if we don't correct this. "You definitely took the insulin?"

He nods and points to the kit, he has always been good at recording his levels and intake. The little book has it written down, and he's taken the correct dosage. This can't be right.

I tell him to drink more juice then pick up the pen which administers his insulin. It looks different to the ones we issue at the clinic.

Jesse has his medication sent to him by us, loaded up with the correct dosage. I don't recognize this brand at all. The pen seems older. My mind scrambles to think of who I dispensed prescriptions for in the last couple of weeks. I don't think I did any for Jesse because he didn't need them yet.

"Where did you get this insulin?" I ask. He leans forward on the counter, sweating even more. I'm on the verge of going into panic mode and getting him to the hospital.

"It came yesterday."

"Yesterday? Jesse, I didn't issue this. Where is the pack you get from the clinic?"

He's not answering. There is no time to do another test and I don't need to. There is no way of knowing how much insulin he's injected without doing proper tests, but if what I suspect is right, he's taken way more than he should have. He needs medical intervention, right now.

Jesse has a car seat for Oscar. I'm too worried to wait for an ambulance. As I move around the counter, I stop in my tracks.

There is a man in the back yard. He's dressed all in black and when he turns, he is wearing a mask. And he has a gun in his hand.

"Jesus," I almost knock everything off the counter.

Jesse looks up and sees the man, he tries to get up. "Oscar," he groans.

I'm caught between the two of them but the man is coming up to the window and there is another one behind him.

"Get Oscar, we have to get to the basement," Jesse stumbles off the chair, holding the counter to keep himself upright. "Go, Taylor. I am okay."

I run across the room as the man starts banging on the door. I can't see him but he is hitting it with some force.

"Hey buddy, we're gonna go downstairs, get Oscar Two okay?" I smile, trying not to show the terror ripping through me.

Thank God he does as he's told. I scoop him up and put a hand over the side of his face to stop him looking at the back door as the man slams against it again. Then another sound come from the front.

Oscar pouts out his lips and looks at me. "Bang."

"Yeah bang. Jesse," I grab his arm to keep him upright.

"Huh," he groans.

"Do you remember how much insulin was in the pen?"

He is really disorientated now and doesn't answer, he lowers his arm and almost drops his phone. I didn't realize he was using it till I see Noah's name on the screen. Jesse keeps mumbling about the basement, but I don't know where that is. I can't trust him to hold Oscar in the state he is in.

We should be getting out of here but I run to the far side of the kitchen.

A bang comes from the front of the house, different to the one from before. My heart practically stops. It was a gunshot.

Dragging a drawer open, I find the glucose tablets and pull them out, spilling other stuff all over the floor. Oscar starts to cry but I don't have time to console him, dragging open a cupboard and pulling out a bag of chips. I hurry back to Jesse and hook my arm under his. He leads us to a door I've never paid attention to before and we go through to a set of stairs.

"Please don't fall," I whisper.

"I'll try," Jesse says, as Noah picks up the call.

"Hey what's up. Why is Oscar crying? Jesse?"

There is a heavy duty bolt on the door which I slam across as a loud bang echoes out in the hallway. They're in the house.

We stumble our way down and Jesse leans against the wall and starts sliding down it. My head swivels around as I try to figure out what we've come down here for.

Jesse raises the phone and I grab it, setting Oscar down trying to calm him. He is feeding off our fear.

"Noah."

"Cherry, what the fuck is going on?"

"There are men here. I don't know who they are."

The other end of the line goes silent for a moment. "Where are you?"

I explain and he tells me to go to the door on the right. I run over and open it only to find another door with a keypad. I tell him and he gives me a code. The men are banging at the basement door now, they can hear Oscar. I turn back to see Jesse crawling over to try to comfort him but he is shaking badly.

"Taylor, the code."

"Okay." I tap it in again and the door opens, revealing a panic room. "Jesus."

"Get inside, hurry up. We're coming."

"Jesse is bad, Noah, he's going into shock. Someone messed with his insulin. I think he's injected way too much."

"Get in the panic room, the door automatically locks. Everything you need is in there, do not come out unless I call Taylor. Go. And Taylor," he pauses. "Protect him."

"I will."

I throw the phone inside and run back for Oscar. He is crying in earnest now as the door above us splinters.

With speed I didn't know I was capable of, I grab Oscar and hurry back to the room. There is a bed in the far corner, I set him down, trying to soothe him and run back out to help Jesse.

"Just get in there," he mumbles.

"I'm not leaving you," I drag him up and he falls against me, almost knocking us over. "Come on Jesse, you can make it."

The door opens and two men come in, running down the stairs. I practically launch us at the door to where the panic room is and push Jesse. He goes sprawling inside as I slam the outer door then get into the panic room. The door closes as the two men get the other door open and raise their guns.

The panic room door slams shut and I hear the faint sound of pinging. The bullets are ricocheting off the metal as some mechanics whir, locking us inside. Oscar is really crying now and I run over to soothe him looking at Jesse on the floor, his whole T-shirt is soaked through with sweat.

"It's okay, honey, we're okay," I press Oscar into my chest and pull the food and tablets from my pocket. "We're gonna go make Uncle Jesse all better okay. He's not feeling so good, do you want to help me?"

He nods, but he's still crying. I wipe his face with the bottom of my t-shirt and kiss his little forehead. I'm not sure how much comfort he is getting but I shuffle off the bed and over to Jesse. He looks up at me with distant eyes.

"We're ok… He's… ok?" He asks.

"We're good, they can't get in." I hope.

The sound of them is faint but they're still there. I set Oscar down and ask him to make sure his puppy is okay, which he does in zero point two seconds, then he reaches for me again.

"Let me do this baby, okay?"

He crawls to Jesse, crying again. Jesse takes his hand and tries to tell him everything is okay as I unwrap a glucose tablet, so thankful Noah keeps everything Jesse needs, I love that about him in that moment.

No matter what anyone says, they will never convince me that Noah is a bad man. Oscar is curling up by Jesse as I give him the tablet, then tear open the chips. His shirt is absolutely drenched but if I don't get more sugar into him he's going to be in serious trouble. If he starts having seizures we're really screwed.

The glucose and food won't be enough to fix this, but it's enough to stop him going into shock. I hope. The phone rings on the floor and I turn around looking for it. It's Noah.

"Are you inside?" he shouts.

"Yes, we're safe. Can they get in here?"

"A tank can't get through those walls, Cherry. Is Oscar okay, I hear him crying," his voice is pained.

"He's a little scared but we're okay." I get up and turn away. "Jesse needs medical help and fast. I don't know what else I can do for him. It's bad, Noah."

"We're almost there. Do you see the screens on the wall? Turn them on for me."

I go over and do as he asks. Three screens turn on showing four different angles on each one, inside and outside the house. There is one right outside the door and a man is there, doing his best to get in, jamming numbers on the keypad. I tell Noah everything I see when he asks, the number of the camera and what is there. Where the men are.

"We're here."

"Be careful."

"Turn off the screens. Do it Cherry, I don't want Oscar to see."

"They're going out the back."

"Good, I have to go. Turn the screens off."

I look up as a man tries to run through the door to the yard, but he falls backwards like a car has hit him. Just before I flick off the screen, Noah steps into view and he runs at the man, jumping on him.

The screens all turn off when I slap the power button and I take a step back. Noah shot that man. I should be in shock but I don't have time for that. They were trying to kill us. They might have killed Jesse. Someone messed with his insulin.

I have no idea if they know about Oscar or if they were going after Jesse, but they weren't expecting me. Not that I've done much. Searching the small room, there is a sink and a door leading to a small toilet. The bed, a fridge which is fully stocked and all the electronics.

Soaking two cloths at the sink I place one on Jesse's forehead to try to bring his temperature down, and then pull Oscar onto my lap as I sit on the ground beside him, talking softly to him as I clear his face of snot and tears. He clutches the puppy between us and I press a hand to the back of his head, holding him close. Jesse is doing his best to eat the chips I'm passing to him.

It's hard to hear anything going on upstairs but there were three men in the house and even though I was watching Noah coming in the back,

I saw his men swarming in on the other cameras. Easily outnumbering them.

Whatever they're doing, they need to do it fast. I'm really scared for Jesse right now and there is literally nothing more I can do to help him.

Chapter Twenty Three

Nero

NOTHING CAN COME CLOSE to the fear and rage pouring through me right now. Hearing Jesse and then Taylor's voice, Oscar screaming in the background. My soul tore out of my body in that single moment as the thoughts ran through my head that I've lost them. All of them.

There is no doubt in my mind who this is.

As we race to my house I curse living so far away. Rebel is in my ear warning us to be careful, it could be another trap but I can't even think about that. Not when I don't know if my family is safe. My bike races ahead of the others but they keep behind me, not letting me do this alone.

Another call comes through from Rebel. "We can't get hold of Gunner."

He's dead, they will have taken him out first. I mourn him for a few seconds then ask Rebel to get off the line so I can call the house. He doesn't argue. We blast through the streets, recklessly swerving to avoid cars. It's a miracle no one is seriously hurt or the cops haven't caught up to us.

None of it matters. The phone rings and rings and I about lose my shit until she answers. She tells me they're safe and even though I can hear Oscar crying, knowing they're in the panic room eases some of the pressure.

That thing cost me nearly thirty grand, but it's fucking worth it, knowing they're protected. Now I can focus everything on the assholes in my home. Going after my son.

Then Taylor says something that scares me. That Jesse is in a bad way. After she has told me what she can see on the camera screens, that there are only three of them, I make sure she turns off the screens as I swerve my bike around the side of the house. I jump off it and it slides across the floor and lands on its side but I don't care.

"Cherry, turn off the camera now."

"Okay."

I hang up and round the back of the house, the door opens, and a man comes through it. He isn't looking at me so when I pull the trigger, he can't escape, and falls back into my house. Adrenalin pushes me on and I burst inside, dropping down and punching the man who is gasping for air. He's wearing a mask, which I rip off. I don't know who he is.

"Where is Storm?" I scream in his face.

"Fuck you."

I grab his head, pull it up and ram it back down on the floor, rattling his fucking teeth and cracking something.

"We have the others. One down, Fury is taking the other one."

"Keep him alive. Where the fuck is Storm?" I shout again, shoving the gun under his chin and punching him in the gut where I shot him. He cries out and blood spurts from his mouth. I hit him again and again.

"Two blocks, east," the man wheezes out. I shoot him and the top of his head blows off.

Rebel grabs my arm before I can run past him. We struggle but he won't let me go. "Razer and Stryker are going. You need to check on them."

"I need to fucking rip his lungs out!" I shout.

"You will, but check on your family."

My heart is pounding and I feel lightheaded. He's right. "We need to get Jesse to the hospital," I tell him, remembering what Taylor said.

Rebel takes out his cell and calls someone. He is yelling them to bring the car around, we need to move Jesse fast. Ronin and Juice come into the kitchen and Rebel tells them to go with me.

My eyes lock with my VP, he nods, letting me know, no matter what, Storm isn't getting away. Pushing past the others I hurry down the stairs to the basement, noting how they've bashed the door down to get to them.

"Motherfuckers," I snarl as I take the stairs two at a time.

The others are behind me as I come to a stop at the door. There are tiny little marks in the metal. This shit is bulletproof. I hope the bullets bounced off and hit the fucker who tried to get in here.

I tap in the code and the door unlocks. When I push inside, Taylor is holding a huge bat, keeping my son and Jesse behind her. The second she sees it's me she drops the bat and starts to cry.

"It's okay, you're safe."

She falls into my arms for a second, then moves back. "Jesse."

Juice moves around me and crouches down, he only gives Oscar a cursory look as I pull my son off the floor and hold him against me. Together they get Jesse up and run out of the room. Oscar is crying again and I hold his face against me with one arm and pull Taylor to me with the other. She presses into my side, her face in my neck.

Fuck. This is all my fault, she could have been killed, and it would have been because of me. Her arm raises and goes around the back of Oscar so she can pull both of us closer. His cries turn to hiccupping whimpers as she strokes his hair.

In that moment, I know the truth of what I've been trying not to admit to myself. I fucking love this woman and no matter the danger, I'm not going to stop and I'm not going to let her go. She got in the way of me and my son, thinking someone was coming in to hurt them, with a baseball bat to protect them. I don't know how I will ever be able to thank her for that.

"Jesse needs the hospital."

"They're taking him." I kiss Oscar's head and cup her face. "Are you okay?"

She nods. "A little freaked out."

"Freaked out," an incredulous laugh bursts out of me. She laughs too. It's fucking fear, nothing else. The relief that none of us are hurt is making us both crazy.

Stryker appears at the door and Taylor lets out a little yelp of surprise and grabs my hand. He looks at her but doesn't say anything, taking in the sight of the child in my arms, a slight furrow of his brow.

"We need to get you out of here," he says.

"Yeah, okay."

"Ratchet will deal with your bike, there is a car waiting."

Taylor doesn't say a word, just does as he asks. We go outside and I'm surprised there aren't more people out here, they've already dispersed, knowing the danger is gone. I help Taylor get Oscar into the car seat, I have no clue how it got there, but I'm not going to question it.

Stryker gets behind the wheel and looks out at me. Rebel is hurrying over and I almost tell Stryker to go without me but I can't leave them.

"Where is he?"

"Gone."

"Fuck." I snap out through gritted teeth.

"We'll find him. Get out of here. The cops are on their way."

My fists clench and a scream of rage and frustration is trying to bust its way out of my chest but I get a hold of it before it can come out. Rebel doesn't stop me when I grab his cut and pull him close, our noses almost touching. He knows I'm not mad at him, he understands the importance of this moment.

"*Find. Him.*"

His face is as deadly serious as mine when he nods, not needing to say anything, his promise is written in the way he stares at me. Then he steps back. "Get the fuck out of here, now," he pushes me toward the open door.

Another beat and I get in as the sound of sirens draw nearer. I'm not getting away from this, it's my house, there is clear evidence it's been broken into and my brothers won't have had time to clean up the mess. Even if there will be no bodies left behind.

None of that matters, we have cops who can help cover up the worst of it.

"Clubhouse?"

I look at Stryker as he pulls away from the curb. Nothing ever phases him and he's driving like he's heading out grocery shopping. At least someone has kept a calm head.

"No," I shake my head and give him a different address.

He doesn't ask me why, or anything about Oscar, just turns the way he needs to go. I can trust him. It has never been up to debate that Stryker isn't fully in with the Disciples. After what he did to Chains, I'll never doubt him.

As he focuses on the road, I turn and look back. Taylor is holding Oscar's hand. He has Oscar Two shoved up against his face which is turned toward Taylor, his eyes are closed. How he is asleep is beyond me.

Taylor looks at me when my gaze goes her way. I'm at a loss for words. I won't force her to stay, or tell her I claimed her so she can't leave.

Her hand lifts, and she reaches out. I turn further and take hold of it. Everything I need to hear, that she won't speak aloud in front of Stryker is said in the way she grips my hand, and my son's.

She isn't going to walk away.

Stryker says no one followed us as we pull up to the address and doesn't show that he knows where we are when we enter the building and take the stairs to the first floor. He's been here before, not too long ago.

We pass the apartment where Ghost's woman used to live. We keep going to the apartment where Caleb Dexter lived. The man who started all of this all those months ago when I realized someone was trying to undercut us.

Those days are long gone. This is no longer about undercutting us. Storm has been threatening for a while but with this, he declared war.

When we forced Caleb to move, I took over the lease on this apartment. It's the last place anyone would ever expect to find me.

Stryker comes in and checks everywhere then waits for me to give him his orders. I nod for him to wait and he goes to stand by the door. Taylor is carrying Oscar and I show her to a bedroom at the back of the apartment. She sets him down and we both look at him after she has pulled the covers over him.

If he was ever going to have bad dreams, this is going to cause it. Taylor touches my hand and I drag my eyes away from my sleeping son.

We slip out but leave the door ajar, going into the other bedroom. She sits down and her head hangs for a moment. I walk closer and stroke her hair so she looks up at me.

"Are you okay?"

"Ask me tomorrow," she quips.

Taking a seat beside her I lift her hand and kiss the backs of her fingers. "If you weren't there..."

"Don't think like that," she whispers.

"But how can you want to be-"

"You warned me, Noah."

"I told you that the club comes first, not that something like this would happen."

"And I told you that I don't care about any of that."

"Jesus, Cherry, you could have died. Because of me."

"But I didn't, because of you. That safe room did exactly what you wanted it to do."

"You shouldn't have to-"

"Can you please not argue with me when I'm trying to tell you that none of it changes how I feel. Yes, I was scared out of my mind. I never doubted you, Noah. You say the club comes first but you're here, with us. You could be out there with them, trying to find this guy Storm."

My lips clamp at his name on her lips. She squeezes my hand.

"It doesn't matter what you try to tell me, or what anyone else says about you, Noah." She lets go of my hand and places it on my chest, right over my heart. "If you were really that man, I wouldn't be able to feel your heart beating, or know that you mean so much to me. Losing me won't happen."

My head is telling me to protest and force her to walk away but she's right. Losing her doesn't work for me either. She shifts her body, turning into me and takes hold of my jaw with her soft fingers, moving me so I'm facing her.

When she kisses me, it's sweet, full of something I've never had with a woman before. Wrapping an arm around her back I pull her closer and open her mouth with my tongue and she lets me, clutching my cut as we kiss harder.

It isn't the kind of kiss that will go any further but it's enough to say she means every word. My phone rings and I sit back. It's Nashville. Taylor nods and I stand up but don't leave the room.

"Jesse is okay, he's on IV meds. They said it's nothing to worry about but his immune system is causing issues."

"Thanks."

We hang up and I fill Taylor in. "That makes sense," she says.

"He'll be okay?" I trust her more than I do what the doctor told Nashville.

"I can't promise you anything," she gets up. "But he's strong. He fought to protect Oscar. With everything he had, he kept him safe."

A ball of emotion swells up my chest and into my throat and she steps into me again, hugging me tight. We stay like that for a few minutes until I kiss her forehead and step back.

Without saying anything she knows. "We'll be okay."

"Stryker will stay with you."

"Maybe I'll invite Dana over."

"No one knows about this place, and it stays that way."

"I was joking."

"You think this is a time for joking, Cherry?" It's said sternly but she sees the twitch in my lips.

"Dana has a thing for Stryker," she whispers, like he is standing outside listening.

Truth is he'll be by the front door and that is where he will stay, all night if he has to. We will need him at some point but for now, there is no one I trust more with these two people I love.

"Tell her to forget it."

"I've tried."

"I mean it. He'll never be what she wants him to be."

Taylor stares at me, reads the seriousness and nods. She promises she will be okay, and I let her know I'll get everything her and Oscar need sent over as soon as I can.

"Noah," she calls as I walk to the door, I turn and look at her. "Don't freak out." She sees my confusion. "I love you. And Nero too."

"We both love you back," I wink at her and it makes me really fucking happy to see that smile.

Only we could say something so damn important to one another that way. Maybe she is in shock and doesn't really mean it. No, Taylor isn't like that. She may have said it that way because of what we went through but it was sincere. I meant it too.

I check in on Oscar one last time, then walk down the hall to Stryker.

"Guard them with your life."

"No need to ask, Prez."

"I'll get Raven to bring some things over for them."

He nods, knowing it's less likely anyone will follow her, but we can trust her. Stryker hands over the keys to the car and steps out of the way to let me pass.

"Oscar might have nightmares," I pause. "He screams. Taylor knows what to do."

He nods, his face stoic. When he first came to us, Stryker never wanted to let anyone know, but I saw it. He suffered with nightmares too. Something has given him PTSD.

He assures me they will all be okay and I head out.

The instant my feet hit the steps down to the lobby, my mind set switches and I harden my head and my heart because I need to.

What I was going to do to Morris for hitting her was bad enough, it's nothing compared to what is coming for Storm.

Once I step outside, I am not a father or a man who told his woman he loves her. I'm the President of the Blackhawk Disciples.

Chapter Twenty Four

Nero

The next time I punch, I think one of my knuckles breaks but I ignore the pain, like I'm ignoring everything else around me. His head lolls forward but I don't give a shit, I hit him again and again, his head moving away and bouncing back straight into my waiting fist.

"He's no good to us brain damaged."

"Shut the fuck up."

"Nero, stop."

I turn to Rebel. "What the fuck did you just say?"

"Whatever I had to, to get you to stop pounding his face into meat. We're not going to find Storm if you fucking kill him. The other two are already dead. This asshole is inner crew, unlike Chains."

Deep down I hear what he is saying but the rage I'd kept bottled up for Taylor and Oscar's sake is finally unleashed. And who better to take it out on than a man who thought it was okay to break into my house, and terrorize my family.

My breath is coming in heavy pants, and my knuckles are thumping with the pain. I can barely make a fist now I've stopped. Looking around the barn, I spot a two by four plank. The only people here are officers, we have everyone out looking for Storm, and making sure the cops aren't on our backs.

"Jesus," Rebel sighs as I point at the plank.

"Fury," I snap.

At least he doesn't question me. He grabs the piece of wood and brings it over. Rebel curses but I ignore him taking the plank. It has a nail in it. Good. Getting a good grip on it, I swing it at his leg. The nail goes into the meat of his thigh making it hard to pull it back, tearing his skin, but it wakes the fucker up and he screams.

"Where the fuck is he?" I scream at him.

"Stop, please, stop."

Fuck this. I pull the gun out of the back of my jeans and fire into the top of his foot. It blows apart, his toes flying in all different directions.

Serves him right for wearing sneakers like a fucking middle schooler. No one is speaking now, not even Rebel. Whatever they're seeing, they won't interrupt. I'm like a fucking animal, I won't deny that is exactly how I feel right now.

Wrapping my hand around his throat, I push him back, making his back arch and bend, and the front legs of the chair lift off the floor.

"Where. The fuck. Is he?" I grind out.

His lips flap and his face is turning blue. Shit, I didn't even feel my hand squeezing around his neck, it's gone numb from punching him so much, my knuckles are swollen and split.

I let him go, and he huffs out and sucks in air, over and over, then coughs when he takes it in too fast. His eyes widen when I point the gun at his groin. He starts groveling again, over and over, begging me not to do it.

Finally reaching his breaking point, he tells us an address. I lower the gun and look at Fury. He smiles and takes the gun and I walk away. I don't give a shit about that guy, all I care about is Storm. All of them head out after me, a gunshot breaks the silence making me pause.

Fury comes out and looks at all of us. We can still hear him screaming.

"What the fuck?" Beast asks, turning as if to go back and finish the job.

"Blew his dick off," he shrugs. "He'll bleed to death before we're half a mile away. In a lot pain."

"Jesus, you're sick," Blaze throws him a dirty look.

"How is that any worse than feeding him to pigs?"

"They're dead when that happens."

"He'll be dead when it happens, having done it slowly, painfully and deserving."

"Shut the fuck up."

Everyone looks at me. I'm all for finding fun in dark places but not tonight. When they all stop and look at me, I take in a deep breath, then exhale. There is no getting away from this.

"You all saw my son tonight. I'm not going to talk about him, who his mom is, or why I've hidden it from you. I did it for a reason and that is all you need to know."

"Why would he go after him?" Rebel lights a cigarette and blows the smoke up in the air. We can still hear the dickless idiot wailing. It's irritating as hell.

"I'm not sure he did. Taylor told me she thought Jesse's prescription had been messed with." I briefly explain his diagnosis and what happened with his medicine. "But he knows about him now."

"We'll protect him with our lives Prez. And Taylor," Nashville says and the others all agree.

"He got away tonight because of the fucking coward he is, hiding away while he sent these men into my house. He might be a chicken shit prick but he isn't stupid. He'll know we grabbed one of his men, and he knows they're not loyal and will give him up without a second thought," I glance at Fury. "Or having his dick blown off."

Nashville grabs his crotch and winces.

"What are you saying?" Rebel steps closer.

Despite what I did in that barn, the rage that tore through me, I see this for what it is. He's slipped through my fingers. The anger, the brutality, that was all for the man who was in my house, who went after my son, my friend… And her. I know they're not going to like hearing this but we'll only end up chasing our tails if we go looking for him now.

"I'm saying," I face my VP. "Chances are he's gone. We're not going to find him at that address. I don't think we're going to find him any time soon. He's lost, every time he's come at us, he's lost. But he's a fucking cockroach," I spit out. "We will never stop looking for him."

"You don't want to go check it out?" Fury asks.

"We'll check it out, but I'm a hundred percent sure he's gone. And he won't stick his neck back out until he thinks he can take us on again."

"What changed?" Rebel asks me. "From that," he points to the barn, which has gone quiet now. "To this."

"Logic. Let's say I'm thinking straighter now that I'm out in the clear air." As if to contradict my words a pig snorts. "I fucking hate it here."

Some of them laugh but Rebel looks irritated, he knows there is more to it than what I'm saying.

"I'll go," Rebel says. "Razer, Beast you're with me, call Ronin to meet us there with Webber and Holdem."

Rebel raises a brow to me, because even though he's my VP and I rarely have a problem with his plans, he still defers to me. I nod. He has to do this, even though my gut is telling me not to waste time.

The three of them head to their bikes. After the sound of the engines dies down, there is another groan from the barn.

"That cockroach analogy applies to everyone around him," Nashville laughs.

"Someone go fucking end him," I sigh.

Fury happily goes back. We don't hear any gunshots and when he comes back, he is wiping blood off a knife, which he puts into the leather roll he carries and tucks in his back pocket.

"If he's gone," Blaze says, stroking a hand through his beard. "What are we going to do?"

"We hunt him." They look around at each other, then back to me. "Whatever way we can. No matter how long it takes. This isn't over. We need to be ready for however he comes back at us."

Blaze frowns.

"What?" I ask him.

"What triggered this? He's been gone for three years, now this?"

"We kicked him out, burned off his patch. He's festered, like the fucking open wound we left on his back," Beast mutters.

"He's right, something happened," I muse, looking across the dusty ground to the outdoor pen. There are two pigs standing there, not doing anything, just staring at one another. "We need to find out what it was. Day and night, until we figure this out. We question anyone who worked with the shitbag, I want to know every move he's made over the last three years, from the second he dragged his sorry ass into the ER to treat that burn."

Everyone agrees.

I don't know how to explain it, but I fully believe Storm has gone to ground. He has failed, after three years of venom filling his bloodstream, he didn't get near us. But he will come back. And we need to be ready.

"We can't leave that mess for Stryker's workers," I pull out my keys.

"Not it, I did it last time," Nashville says holding a hand up.

"Pussy," Fury shakes his head.

"They creep me the fuck out. You ever heard them crunching bones. That shit is fucking obscene."

"Where is a prospect when you need one," Blaze laughs.

Anyone watching this would think we're insane, but this is who we are.

They don't think any less of the situation, they know how grave it is and how pissed I am but they understand that sometimes, we need to let it out in different ways.

Do I hate that I am not going to get at Storm now, damn fucking right I do, but I will get him. Rebel still thinks we can catch up with him, and he'll go at it for as long as it takes to convince him otherwise.

"I don't care who, someone do it. Nashville, I'm going to check on Jesse, you're with me."

I pretend not to notice when he flips them off and follows me.

Nashville waits in the hallway while I go into the private room where they're keeping Jesse. He may be loaded, but I'm not exactly living on the breadline. I stand by the side of his bed for a long time, looking down into the face of my best friend.

If anyone other than Taylor was there today, he'd be dead. And without Jesse, I would never have met her.

I stay for an hour, then head outside. Nashville is busy chatting up a nurse, but he walks away, with a wink and a smile. That shit comes easy to him.

"Speedway called," he says as we make our way out of the hospital.

"What he say?"

"He's pissed he wasn't there."

"If he had been, he'd likely be dead."

Nashville lowers his head. I haven't forgotten that one of our brothers was killed today, last night... I can't remember what fucking day it is anymore. The sun is lightening as we leave the hospital. Gunner's death won't be forgotten, it adds to the list of things Storm will pay for.

"Fuck I'm tired," I rub my forehead.

"It's been a rough twenty-four hours."

I blow out a sigh. "What else did Speedway say."

"He said call him when you get a chance. Where to now?"

Nashville won't ask, even though he sees there is an underlying tension.

"You can head back to the clubhouse, or home or whatever."

He pauses and leans back against a metal balustrade on the ramp for wheelchairs. "Anyone know where you're going?" he tilts his head to look out at the parking lot.

"Stryker."

"Good," he looks back. "Then I'm gonna go to the strip club," he grins, straightens up and slaps my arm. "But first let me see you to your bike."

"Fuck off." I punch him and he laughs.

I'm starting to feel the tiredness as I make my way to the apartment in Canton. Just as I approach the tattoo shop the door opens and my brother steps out taking a cigarette from behind his ear. His head lifts at the sound of the bike and our eyes meet.

I never let him join the MC, but I did teach him how to ride. He's been ignoring me for weeks now. Might as well deal with this shit too.

He isn't too surprised when I pull over, stow my helmet and walk toward him.

Phoenix doesn't look anything like me. He takes after his mother with her dark hair and green eyes. The fucker is so good looking, he had club whores panting after him before he was even legal. With all the tattoos and piercings, the cigarette and dark clothes, I'm surprised he doesn't have an endless stream of women in and out of his bed.

My brother isn't like that. I'm glad about that.

"Thought you quit," I indicate the cigarette as he cups his hands around it and lights it, inhaling deeply.

"It didn't stick."

Through the window the dark-haired girl covered in tattoos is watching us. I'm pretty sure Phoenix was dating her for a while but they're not together now. There is no one else in there that I can see.

"Garrett is in Texas," he says.

I nod. Phoenix huffs a laugh. I don't say anything in response to his silent suggestion I'm keeping tabs on them.

"What are you doing around here?"

"Some shit went down last night, things got messy."

"And you're here to tell me what? To watch out for something?"

"No, you can take yourself Phoenix." He eyes me, taking a drag on the cigarette. "I have a kid."

His mouth pops open and for the first time he loses some of that hard built-up composure and bravado he shows around me. "Like, a kid?"

"He's two, his name is Oscar. I've kept him a secret to protect him but I realize now that was a bad idea. He isn't going to be like me."

"Why are you telling me this?" he asks, dropping the cigarette and stomping on it to make sure it's out. Then he bends down and pockets the stub. This is the kind of man my brother is.

"If you want to get to know him."

"Do you want me to get to know him?"

A car drives by slowing and I watch it, making sure.

"Don't be cryptic with me, Nero. I'm beyond that shit. And the only reason I'm giving you the time of day is because of what you did for Garrett."

He doesn't mean letting him out of his obligations to the club, he's referring to Garrett's sister.

"He needs good role models."

"You think that's me?" he laughs.

"Yes."

The laughter stops and he stares at me, trying to figure me out. After a few seconds he blinks out of whatever he went into. "His name's Oscar? Who's the mom?"

"Not important."

"Meaning you're not with her?"

"Meaning it's complicated. There is another reason I stopped."

"You stopped cos you saw me coming out, you didn't intend to come here."

"I didn't think you'd want to do me the favor, but no harm in asking."

"What favor," he looks through the window, so I do too, the little dark-haired girl has her arms crossed as she watches us. I'm not touching that problem. He wouldn't want me to ask.

"A tattoo."

"For you?"

"A woman."

His brow lifts. He knows what I'm saying. He grew up around the MC, comes to the parties occasionally, or used to, before shit went sideways with his best friend.

"I want you to meet her."

"Your son and your woman, must be my birthday."

He walks past me and heads to the door. There aren't a lot of people who would dare to walk away from me like that. Phoenix is one of the few who gets away with it. He always has.

I love this kid, whether he likes it or not. I've kept him at arm's length to protect him, to allow him to live this life he loves here at Blackhawk Ink.

"Bring her by Tuesday, around nine. I have free time." He doesn't look back as he goes in the shop.

It's a start.

Might as well get all the shit over and done with before I go back to Taylor. Speedway asks about Oscar, wanting to know his nephew is okay, which I confirm, telling him it's unlikely he'll remember it and we don't need to worry.

"Where the fuck is Sheridan?"

"Fucking Kentucky. Went to visit a friend."

I'm too tired to care. "When is she coming back?"

"That's the thing," he says sounding pissed. "She said she isn't. Said Oscar is safe with you so you can keep him."

"What?"

He explains she met a guy, and they're eloping and she doesn't want Oscar, sounding defeated.

"I'll keep trying Prez."

"Don't bother. She's already lost any right to him."

"She's his mom."

"A mother doesn't say someone can *keep him* and come back from that, Speedway. I know she's your sister, but she is dead to me after that."

"Shit, Nero, come on."

"I've had a long fucking night, I'm tired and I've been away from my son too long after what he went through. We'll talk when you get back but it's gonna take a lot to change my mind."

The ride to the apartment is only a few blocks from the tattoo shop, I park round the back and go in that way, texting Stryker to let him know I'm on my way up. He greets me at the door, tells me everything is fine, then leaves.

I round the corner to Taylor sitting on the floor showing Oscar how to tie his shoelace. How can she have known him only a few weeks and look like more of a mother than his own? I'll wrap my head around that shitshow another day. Right now, I feel like I'm going to pass out.

"Dada," Oscar gets up and moves like a rocket towards me. I lean down and scoop him up, reveling in the smell of baby shampoo in his hair.

Taylor turns and gets up, watching me silently. I walk over and drop onto the couch, holding Oscar in my lap. He is chattering away but my eyes are on her.

"You need sleep."

"Not yet. I need to be with you both."

She eyes my swollen knuckles but doesn't say anything, just goes to the bathroom and comes back with a first aid kit. It's a miracle neither of them have even a scratch on them.

With Oscar's sometimes unhelpful help, Taylor gets me cleaned up and I have bandages wrapped around my whole hand, but I don't care because Oscar is smiling and laughing. I know kids are resilient but seeing him like this means everything to me.

We watch TV and I somehow fall asleep. Taylor wakes me up when she has put Oscar down for a nap and forces me into the shower, then bed.

"Hey," I grab her hand before she can leave and tug lightly but enough to knock her off balance so she falls beside me. "Are you okay?"

It's obvious she is going to give me some platitude so I will get some rest but that won't fly with me and she sees it written in the way I'm watching her.

"I was scared, for Jesse and Oscar and me," she adds quietly. "But I knew you were coming."

"What if I don't get there next time?"

"There will be a next time?" she asks.

"He got away." I'm not going to lie to her about that. "We'll find him and I'll make sure he can't hurt you, or anyone else in the club."

"You'll take on all of that responsibility?"

"It's my job."

Her eyes flick back and forth on mine. It's on the tip of my tongue to say she still can make a different choice, I won't stop her.

"You need to sleep," she leans down and presses her lips to mine, brushing a hand over my hair. "I'll be here when you wake up."

"I don't deserve you. I'm not going to let you go, Cherry."

"Good job I don't intend to go anywhere then. Now go to sleep, you can save the world tomorrow."

I laugh half-heartedly, and with great effort.

Taylor turns off the lamp, it's still light in here but my eyelids are drooping. I fall asleep to the sound of her breath and her hand stroking over my hair.

Chapter Twenty Five

Taylor

As soon as Noah is in a deep sleep, I go back into the living room and tidy everything up. I won't tell him I've barely slept myself, how could I when he was out there chasing after a monster? And the man he left to watch over us was scary as hell. How Dana was ever attracted to him, I have no idea.

At least that is what I thought when Noah first left us here with him. He stood by the door guarding it for nearly three hours before I took him a chair and a can of coke from the fridge. It was another hour before he actually sat.

Then Oscar got interested and walked out into the hall to watch him. The first few times I brought him back to the living room, then I watched. After everything we'd been through the kid fearlessly walked up to where Stryker was sitting and held out his puppy, telling him the dogs name.

Stryker looked down at him and Oscar stared back. Then he sat on the floor and babbled at him. It looked like he wasn't paying any attention, but they were both happy enough, so I went to make something to eat.

All of this took my mind off what is going on. I was worried about Noah and what he was doing, I couldn't stop thinking about Jesse, even though they told me he was safe at the hospital and being treated. And I intended to do everything I could to keep Oscar safe and happy.

If that meant watching him talk nonsense to a giant man who looked like he ate toddlers for breakfast, who was I to stop it.

Then Oscar started to cry, and I hurried out into the hall. Stryker was helping him up and checking his head. From the gentle way he handled him, I guessed Oscar fell over. He's good at walking but he's a little clumsy. Stryker set him on his feet and handed him his puppy, then sat back down. Oscar stopped crying and after a few moments of contemplation, he sat down beside the chair, closer this time.

Stryker looked up and caught me watching and gave a simple nod, then went back to being the silent protector.

That's when I figured out what Dana could actually like about him. Her attraction is to the fighter, she doesn't know this side of him, I doubt many people do.

Then Raven showed up with things that both of us would need. Some of it was from my house.

"Did you really think he didn't have a key?" she asked at my confusion then laughed at my irritation. "He's gonna be all up in your business now, honey. Speaking of which," she lifted a bag, made sure Oscar and Stryker weren't paying any attention and tossed it to me.

My cheeks burned so hot I almost threw the bag back at her as she laughed. It had red lacy lingerie inside.

"You're welcome," she told me.

It was nice to have her here, she took my mind off everything that kept threatening to consume me. She was good with Oscar too, saying no one had any idea he existed.

When I asked if she knew who the mom might be she said no, but she looked at Oscar for a long time after that, giving me the impression she was figuring it out.

"When Nero's ready, he'll tell you."

It's odd hearing people call him that. It happened a lot last night. He was that man last night, and I was glad of it. For a while I struggled with the memory of him shooting someone but rationalized it to keep myself from getting too caught up. That was the man who burst into the basement, who ran at me, trying to get to us, who shot the door of the panic room.

They tried to kill Jesse by tampering with his medication.

The fridge has plenty of food and Raven brought more when she came. It's getting late so I decide to cook dinner. To keep my mind active. I'll have to wake Oscar up soon or he won't sleep tonight.

When did this happen? When did I start worrying about someone else's son? It comes naturally. He's a part of Noah. One who will always be around. I'm glad I got to know him before this happened, he trusts me.

"Hey," Noah comes up behind me. "What are you busy thinking about out here?"

"You should be asleep."

"I got a couple of hours."

"It's not enough."

He wraps his arms around my waist and buries his face in my hair. I still and let him wrap himself around me. I'm starting to see that Noah needs to have this side of him, when he's away from the club, with Oscar. With me.

His hand moves upwards, and he cups my breast.

"What are you doing?"

"Just making sure you're okay?"

"You're making sure *this* is okay?" I indicate where his hand is.

"Yeah," he kisses my neck and slips his hand under the T-shirt, tugging down the bra so he can pinch my nipple. "Making sure you're here. You're safe."

My head tilts back to his shoulder. This is really not the time, but I don't stop him. He lowers his other hand and slides it inside my pants.

"Here too," he murmurs, one finger pressing inside. "This feels very real," he nips my earlobe making me moan.

I have to set down the knife I'm holding and grab onto the counter as he teases my nipple and pushes another finger inside me. He works his fingers faster and whispers for me to be quiet, which is almost impossible when he thrusts his hard cock against me.

"You're mine, Cherry. No one is ever going to hurt you as long as I'm alive."

"Don't say that," I shake my head, coming out of the lust induced haze.

"It's true." He pushes his hips against mine, rocking us back and forth. "Be quiet now," he kisses my neck, biting where it meets my shoulder as he starts finger fucking me harder.

I want to protest, tell him the thought of him dying tears my insides apart but he doesn't stop and I turn my head to kiss him as the climax builds.

"Want to fuck you so bad, but this is all we can do, Cherry. For now. Making you come, hearing you moan for me, it's the sweetest sound. Come for me, now. Do it, come."

No man has ever said anything like this to me and it's not like I can come on command. Except I am and I bite down hard on my lip to stop me crying out too loud. He strokes me through it, his hand still over my breast. It moves between them and he taps where my heart is beating faster.

Holding onto the counter is the only thing keeping me steady as he backs away. I turn around as he slips his fingers into his mouth and my knees go weak as he licks them, his eyes on me.

"Dada, your here."

"Shit," he runs a hand over the back of his jeans and steps around me as I turn away to get myself back together.

"Hey buddy," he crouches down and Oscar runs over for a hug.

The way he is holding him is equal parts beautiful to see and funny because he's keeping him away from the arousal he's trying to hide. He stands up and holds Oscar tight, giving him a hug, until his son protests and tells us he's hungry.

"Me too," Noah looks over at me when he says it. Jesus, this man.

"When we go home?" he asks.

"Soon." I glance over. "That's our home, Cherry. I'm not letting anyone push us out. But work will be done on it first. It's safe here, for now."

He goes off to get Oscar and himself washed up for dinner. He is right, *for now*. There will be a time when I tell him I'm not leaving dad's house, not yet and I have to go back to work, but that can wait. He needs time to wrap his head around what happened. To know we're all safe.

And I need that too. Just for a little while. It was hard not knowing where he was all night but his words from all those weeks ago play around in my head. Only now, I don't fully believe him. Maybe his club does come first, but when it mattered, he dropped everything and came for us.

It drove me crazy thinking maybe I'm on the peripheral, a bystander, he was only coming for his son, but he's proved to me that isn't the case.

Having a man like him love me means life is going to be different to what I've known before. He meant what he said, he's shown me how he feels. My insecurities are mine to deal with.

Work let me take a couple of days off but then I do have to go back. Noah isn't happy, but he says it's okay so long as I have someone watching me. He introduced me to a guy named Holdem. They have the oddest names.

When I asked, he said he was from Texas. Like that makes sense, until he pointed out it was a form of poker and he's really good at it.

Not moving into the house with him when it was ready a week later caused a... disagreement. I wouldn't say argument as such. He said I had to, I told him no, he got all silent and broody for an hour, and I refused to back down. Then he told me Blaze was going to kit out dad's house with a full security system and Holdem was going to be my shadow. He wouldn't hear any argument about it.

I agreed.

Dana is the only one of my friends I told the full story to. She was pissed as hell and demanded to meet Noah, giving him a piece of her mind about protecting me or he'd have to deal with her. He'd looked at her like she was a minor inconvenience he could forget about as soon as she left, but he heard her out, because she is my best friend.

Everything she was demanding he'd already promised to do, neither of us told her that. She left feeling as if she got one over on him and I love him for allowing her to believe that.

Noah isn't fully on board with having Oscar around the club but when he is there, all the guys dote on him, but there is only one of them he is interested in.

He follows Stryker around like a tiny shadow. After a while, he started picking him up. They didn't talk, but they had an odd understanding that no one else could figure out.

While he is being entertained, Noah pulls me aside and takes me upstairs.

"I want you to meet my brother," he says, as we go into the bedroom.

"Haven't I met them all?"

"My biological brother. He's a few years younger than me, works in a tattoo shop in Canton. I had planned to take you there sooner but with everything going on I had to put it off."

He sees my frown at not knowing about this and guides me to the bed. "He's my half-brother, and I have spent most of his life keeping away from the club. It worked so well, he kinda hates me now."

"That can't be true."

"I want to fix it. I've let him down in the past, been the asshole when I had to be, for his own good. A couple of times I've not been there for him. It's time that changed. He also agreed to do it."

"To rebuild the relationship?"

"No, well, hopefully. But I mean the tattoo."

"You're getting another tattoo?" He stares at me until I get his meaning. "Me?"

"Yeah, it's kind of a thing."

"What does that mean?"

He grins at me. I've never wanted a tattoo, and I don't want one now.

"You'll come round, Cherry," he cups my face and turns it to him. "You're a part of the club now."

"Is this some kind of MC ritual?"

He smirks and I roll my eyes. A tattoo is insane, it's permanent. As he stares into my eyes, I melt a little, he has a way of doing that. I'm not a pushover though, he knows he can't order me around the way he does with his men.

He pulls me up and stands me in front of him, running his hands up my thighs. It's not so easy for us to be alone lately, with Oscar coming to live with him full-time.

He explained his mom took off and wasn't coming back. It hurt to think a woman could leave her child like that and Noah was pissed for a while but now he's happy.

It means we have to be careful, and then I'm still at my place a lot of the time. I'm really not ready to let go of my dad's home. Not yet.

"Strip."

I glower at him, but it doesn't last long. When I step back and start removing my clothes, Noah slides off the bed and sits on the floor, watching me with hooded eyes. He crooks his finger when I'm fully naked for him and I walk over, placing my feet on either side of his thighs.

Seeing him in his cut used to make me nervous, now it makes me hot. He leans forward and presses his nose against my pubic bone, running his hands up the back of my thighs, he tugs me closer.

"You remember the first time I did this?" His tongue probes inside of me, then he pulls back.

It's taking everything in me not to fall down.

"You told me you didn't like it, Cherry." He flicks at my clit making me jolt and grab his shoulders. "Said you couldn't come from having your pussy licked."

"I remember," I breathe out.

"You don't believe that anymore, do you?"

God no. I shake my head and move my hips slightly, making him laugh against my hot skin. I'm so wet, it's starting to run down my inner thigh.

"You smell like fucking heaven," he brings one hand around and uses his thumb and forefinger to spread me open, staring so intently it should embarrass me. Nothing this man does embarrasses me anymore. "Hold on tight, Cherry, I'm going to make you come so many times you'll forget your name." He licks me from the bottom of my pussy up to my clit, making me whimper. "But never my name. Right, Cherry." He pinches my clit making me cry out.

"No, Noah."

"Fuck my face, Cherry," he growls, never being able to resist hearing me breathe out his name. "Show me how fucking much I've made you love this."

I push my hips at his face and he spears his tongue into me. He doesn't stop till I've fallen apart twice for him, barely able to stand but his strong hands on my waist kept me upright.

He is staring up at me, his face is soaked and his eyes are hooded as he strokes a finger inside my thigh, through the wetness.

"Here," he says, his eyes still on me.

"What?" I ask, still half dazed.

"This is where you'll have my name tattooed on you."

"What?" That snaps me out of the haze.

"Every time I lick this pussy till you break, I will see my name."

"Wait a minute."

"Nope." He grabs my hips and spins me around, getting up and walking me over to a bureau.

"Noah," I protest.

"Exactly," he undoes his jeans and thrusts inside me.

"You can't... use... sex to make... me... ohhh." The words fall out of my head as he fucks me in that way he knows how to scramble my brain. He has me wrapped around his finger. Or his cock.

Maye it won't be so bad having his name on me.

"So long... as you have... mine."

He grips my hips and pushes in and out of me, making my words stutter, then presses his lips to my ear. "It will be right where every motherfucker can see it, Cherry. So they all know," he thrusts harder and stops, holding there so he's all I can feel, in and around me.

I fully expect him to say '*your mine*' he says it often enough, mostly while we're having sex. But he surprises me this time.

"I'm yours, Cherry, and I always will be."

Epilogue

Nashville

“FUCK YEAH, THAT’S GOOD.”

I close my eyes and rest my head against the leather seat back, one hand on my thigh, the other on the back of the woman’s head. I haven’t got a clue what her name is, she is one of the dancers here at Elegance. That’s what they’re called. Plain truth is, they’re strippers. It is a strip club after all.

It’s upscale though, so we call them dancers.

The last twenty-four hours have been a total head fuck. I still can’t believe Storm got away from us, a fact confirmed by Rebel after I left the Prez. I still don’t know how he manages to predict these things, but Nero has never been wrong.

I’m drawn out of those thoughts when the woman cups my balls and I thrust my hips a little harder. This isn’t expected of the dancers here but now and then, they give a little extra during a lap dance, for a small fee. Officers in the club don’t have to deal with that but I’ll give her something because she is practically sucking the flesh off my cock, in a good way.

I don't fuck them, but the occasional blow job gets out some of the tension that comes along with being a part of the Blackhawk Disciples. And it's been a hell of a time lately.

"Fuck," I groan as she uses both hands, stroking me up and down and squeezing my balls, her mouth bobbing up and down faster. I bite down on my cheek as I come, she takes it all then sits back on her heels and looks up at me. It takes a moment to get my breath back.

"Thanks sweetheart," I cup her chin. "Anyone ever tell you you're an expert at that?"

"All the time," she presses her palms on my knees to help her up.

That kind of takes away from the moment, but I did ask. In this line of business, she isn't going to be coy about sex.

And without a care in the world, she's butt ass naked in a pair of red heels that made me choose her when I got here looking for something to take the edge off. Her pussy is glistening but I'm done for now. I tuck my dick back in my pants and she takes a step back when I stand.

I watch her grab a robe from the hook by the door, slip her arms in and walk back out into the club, not even bothering to tie the sash so she's fully on show.

That is the only kind of woman I can deal with right now. The ones who do what needs to be done and walk away without questioning me. And I do feel a hell of a lot more relaxed as I walk back into the bar. It's quieter because it's mid-afternoon but there are still some men in the booths, a couple of dancers up on the stage.

Beast is sitting at the bar and eyes me as I walk over and ask the bar tender for a beer. He sets it in front of me and heads to a waitress holding a tray. She's wearing the uniform of the wait staff, an apron that about covers her tits and booty shorts that show off a lot of cheek.

I've never seen her before. Beast catches me looking and glares.

"New girl, started a couple of nights back."

He manages Elegance and is in charge of all the new hires, wait staff, dancers and everything in between. Beast isn't the kind who shits where he eats, but he does eye the new girl with a strange look.

"What's that look for?" I ask.

"She wants to dance, but isn't old enough. What's so fucking funny?"

"Your morals."

"I take care of our girls."

That's true. I drink some more beer and watch her walk toward us, keeping the tray steady as she goes. It looks like one false move and she'll drop the whole thing. She's like Bambi, all long legs and huge eyes.

She turns our way as she gets closer and her eyes widen when she looks at me, then her cheeks flush the color of ripe strawberries.

"And that means you stay the fuck away."

"You know I was back there getting my cock sucked, right?"

A crash behind us has us both turning around. She's dropped everything on the floor.

"How good of a dancer is she?" I laugh. "Because she is a shit server. Nice ass though," I note when she bends down to clean up.

Ellie, one of our long-term dancers, walks over and looks down at her, then over to Beast with an elegant arch of her brow. He flips her off and turns back to his drink, so I do the same, minus the rude hand gesture. It's not of any interest for me to get involved but as she straightens up and talks in a low whisper to Ellie, I can't help but watch.

"How old is she exactly?"

"Get fucked Calum."

"The real name," I grin at him.

"Stay away from my staff."

"Didn't we just have this exact conversation?"

"Where is Nero?" he changes the subject.

"Stryker's with him." That sobers my mood.

"Good. This shit with Storm is messed up."

I couldn't agree more. "What's even more messed up is Nero having a kid no one knew about," I say quietly.

He might have shared the news with us, that doesn't mean we're going to gossip about it where strangers could hear.

"Nope, having an old lady is the real fucking surprise."

I laugh but don't let on I've known about Taylor for a while. It was me Nero sent to make sure her house was secure early on. No man does that for just any woman.

"Last few weeks has been full of them."

"All the more reason to be vigilant," he reminds me, although he doesn't have to.

Nero is a good President. He's never done anything to have any of us doubt him. We will always have his back, even if it means dying for him. Hopefully that never happens to any of us. Although we lost a good guy.

And Chains. Fuck, things are getting messy. We thought we could get on top of the shit with Storm but a strange foreboding is growing in my gut. Not knowing where the cunt is, or what he is going to do next is worrying.

I tap the bar and get up. "I'm going home to sleep for two days."

"Good luck with that."

"Be careful, yeah."

Beast flips *me* off and I laugh turning to walk away. I catch the little blond as she is about to go through the door to the back. Guess Ellie took her off wait duty. I'm not sure she'll last. There is something too innocent about her, like she doesn't belong here.

Now that I'm really looking at her, she's fucking beautiful.

Beautiful women are dangerous. *Young* beautiful women even more so. It's a full on bad idea to talk to her, never mind watch her ass wiggle as she slips through the door.

I try to put her out of my mind as I ride back to my apartment. The innocent wide-eyed look keeps popping into my mind's eye. All that creamy smooth skin of her ass, and the side of her full, high tit when she reached for the broken bottles.

Fuck, she's already trouble. It's best I stay the hell away from Elegance, at least until Ellie fires her, which is inevitable. A girl like that doesn't belong around us.

The sooner she realizes that, the better.

Acknowledgements

Thank you so much for reading. If you have enjoyed Nero, please consider leaving a review, these really help indie authors and also readers when checking out their next TBR addition!

I'm excited about this series, and knew I always wanted to explore the brother of Phoenix from the Blackhawk Ink series as soon as he was introduced. This is going to something I've never done before with a 10-book series that has a storyline running through all the books.

I'd like to thank my betas, Sandra and Karen as ever for their help, particularly the medical knowledge that really helped having a nurse on the team. To all the ARC readers for this one, I was blown away by how many people ARC read this one and thank each and every one of them for wanting to support me and the Blackhawk Disciples.

To my family as always for their love and support. And as ever, a great big thanks to you, the READER. Thank you so much for reading Nero and I hope you're ready for what is coming with the rest of the brothers of the Blackhawk Disciples.

Also by Chris Reilly

The Devil's Chaos Duet:
Devil's Chaos
Devil's Daughter
Devil's Falling

Novellas:
Devil's Desire
Devil's Kiss

BreakNeck Series:
Sky Full of Stars
Touch in the Dark
The Sounds of Her
Perfect Storm

Spin-Off Novellas:
Standing Still
Fight For Forever

Sports Romance:
Off The Line

Red Alert Series:
Electric Touch
Midnight Heat

Standalone Romance:
Reckless

Christmas Eve, Eve
Undone, Love Times Three

Blackhawk Ink Tattoo Series
Broken

Blackhawk Disciples MC
Nero
Nashville

About The Author

I was born and raised in Liverpool, UK and loved to read from as early as I can remember. Writing came along when I was about 13-14 and English and essay writing (creative obviously) became my favorite lesson! I currently live with my son and two cats.

The majority of my 20's/30's I read thrillers. Both mysteries and detective-based books. I made the switch to romance when I picked up a book called 'Dirty Letters' I loved it and the authors so much, I went looking for more. I then went down the rabbit hole of Indie Romance and was amazed and inspired by these amazing authors.

Happily ever after is always the goal for my characters, but there may be a cliff-hanger or two, and definitely some angsty situations to work through, occasionally a little bit dark, but oh so delicious.

www.ingramcontent.com/pod-product-compliance
Lightning Source LLC
LaVergne TN
LVHW020044110826
845155LV00029B/629

* 9 7 8 1 9 1 9 4 5 4 0 0 9 *